REAP THE WHIRLWIND

Keri hadn't expected her father to leave her anything, least of all a half share in a hotel in Switzerland. And she didn't know anything at all about the man who owned the other half, Paul von Hasler. She was soon to find out, though . . .

REAP THE WHIRLWIND

BY

ANNE HAMPSON

MILLS & BOON LIMITED
17–19 FOLEY STREET
LONDON W1A 1DR

First published 1975
This edition 1976

© Anne Hampson 1975

ISBN 0 263 71905 7

Made and Printed in Great Britain by
Richard Clay (The Chaucer Press), Ltd., Bungay, Suffolk

CHAPTER ONE

THE taxi sped on through an enchanted region where there could be found every combination of mountain scenery—glaciers and massive peaks, high cascades and shining ribbon lakes, snow-capped horns and spires.

Keri Hartnell sat surveying all this, but her mind was busy trying to focus a mental picture of the man she was soon to be confronting—Paul von Hasler whom she had not seen for ten years and who was now her business partner. The picture eluded her; what did appear with startling clarity was a very different picture, and one which Keri had not the least desire to recall! For she had on that particular occasion suffered the supreme indignity of her life. And it had been at the hands of Paul, who was then only twenty years of age.

'Sow the wind and you'll reap the whirlwind,' Keri's grandmother used to warn her when, so very often, Keri would get up to some of her tomboy tricks. Well, she had reaped the whirlwind on that particular occasion and no mistake! However, the imperious Paul von Hasler would soon discover that he had a confident young woman to deal with now, not a small, defenceless child of twelve.

'That is the Castle Raimegen—up on the hill over there.' The taxi-driver flicked a hand, then returned his attention to the road. 'It was once a private residence, but it's now an hotel, as you know. I expect you're staying there for a holiday?'

Having no desire to correct the man Keri said nothing. She remembered the castle well, for to a girl of twelve it had been a veritable fairy-tale castle. Standing majestically on a flat-topped hill, it had not changed at all. Old and moated, it was surrounded by beautifully-wooded parklands, with breathtaking Alpine scenery rising behind, and the deep valley falling away in the other direction, sloping down to the delightful and unspoiled village of Wilderswil in the Bernese Oberland district of Switzerland. This was such another day as that on which Keri had first seen it, with its white walls and bright red pointed turrets gleaming in the sunshine. On that particular day she had her father with her, her father whose partner in the hotel business at that time was Herr Max von Hasler, Paul's father. Now both men were dead and their children owned the flourishing concern which involved no fewer than eleven hotels in various parts of the country.

'We shall not be long now.' They were passing through Wilderswil's enchanting main street and Keri found herself trying to remember something about it. But all that she could remember was the castle itself; it was there again when they had left the village behind, standing proudly on the hill, a patrician of rare quality and design ... and it was half hers! Something sang within her. She had been kept so poor by a miserly father whose wife had long since left him and gone off to America with her new husband. Keri had been forced to work in an office, earning her own keep and with never a cent coming to her from her father. As she grew up she often wondered what had possessed him, on that one solitary occasion, to spend the money to

6

take her with him to Switzerland.

'We're here at last!' Keri spoke to herself, her nerves becoming unsteady now, but with excitement more than anything else. 'What's wrong?' she asked, speaking louder now so that the driver could hear her. 'Can't we get into the driveway?' A long luxury coach was standing right across the entrance and although the high wide gates were swung open the driver found it impossible to get through the narrow space at the front of the coach. Stopping his taxi, he got out; a moment later he was telling Keri that the coach had broken down and that she would have to get out and walk the length of the drive.

'That's all right,' she returned cheerfully. 'The luggage, though—it's a long way for you to carry it.'

'I'll manage. I can make two journeys.'

Keri said she was sorry about this, but as the man didn't seem to mind the inconvenience she began to walk up the drive. High trees growing on both sides met overhead, while all over the lawns summer flowers grew in abundance. The castle dominated the entire scene; Keri could not help wondering what it would be like to have it for a home instead of it being an hotel. It would be altogether too vast, she decided, her eyes falling on a beautiful white chalet visible through some flowering trees and bushes away across at the far side of the castle grounds. Who lived there? she wondered, thinking she herself would not mind something similar. For the present, though, she was to live at the hotel, just until she could sort out her position with Paul von Hasler who had been her father's partner for over six years, his own father having died when Paul was only twenty-four. Mr Hartnell had then made his home in Switzerland, telling Keri that, at sixteen, she was well able to take care of herself. Keri had long ago suspected that her father would leave all his wealth to charity, and having resigned herself to this she was astonished to be told, on his death, that he had failed to leave a will.

'You are an extremely wealthy young lady,' the lawyer had told her. 'What are you going to do? Sell out to this Swiss gentleman, as he has asked you to?'

'Yes, I think so.'

'It's a wise decision, Miss Hartnell. You can then invest your money.'

Invest it ... Keri had no idea about investments and the more she thought about selling out to Paul, the stronger became the conviction that she could do a great deal worse than leave things as they were. Why go to all the trouble of selling out, then have to go through the headache of finding safe investments? Her money *was* invested, so why not leave it like that? When informed of her decision Paul had not been pleased and because of this Keri had hesitated a long time before deciding to go to Switzerland. But two circumstances had combined to bring about her decision finally. First, she had been made redundant owing to the firm's merger with another, larger company. And although Keri could now well afford to be independent of a job, she could not see herself living a life of idle luxury. The second circumstance which made its contribution to her decision was the memory of Switzerland—its mountains and valleys, its cleanness and its charming friendly people. These she remembered; they had made a deep impression on her when she was at a most impressionable age. She had often since then asked her father to take her again, but he had never had any time for her at all. She had been put into the

8

care of his housekeeper until, of course, the time when he had decided to sell up his home in England and settle in Switzerland.

He had not wanted Keri with him—she was too much like her mother, he had once said, and he had no wish to be constantly reminded of the wife who had deserted him—and so she had been forced, at only sixteen years of age, to set herself up in a flat, where she had lived alone for the next five and a half years. Her father had died six months ago and Keri's whole prospect regarding the future had changed. She was rich. And as she and her father had never had anything in common, she did not even have to endure the suffering which almost always follows the loss of a parent. As for her mother—Keri did not even know whether she was alive or dead. She could not even remember her, but she never condemned her, for she must have had a most unhappy life with her first husband who was both miserly and totally without any of the finer qualities which are necessary in a husband and father. With Keri he was often icily domineering—like a Victorian father, his housekeeper would often declare. Nevertheless, Keri possessed a brave streak that helped her ride her father's domination to some degree. It was not only a brave streak, but also a mischievous one, and without doubt she was a tomboy when she was young. This mischievous streak was, her father maintained, a vice she had inherited from her mother; it was the taint of evil, he said, and it was because of this that Keri had fully believed he would disinherit her. Even now, when she dwelt on it, she found it incredible that he had not made a will leaving everything away from her.

Her musings about the past came to an end as she

9

reached the fork in the long drive which, she remembered, led to the front of the castle if one took the left-hand path, and to the back if one took the right-hand path. Or was it the other way round? She stood a moment, undecided. Yes, she was almost sure the left-hand path went to the imposing front entrance....

'What does it matter which way I go in?' she said a trifle impatiently. 'I'm not a guest!'

And so she wandered along the path which she thought would come out at the front, but in fact it did prove to be the one that came to the back entrance. However, Keri recalled that there was a long passageway just to the right as one entered and this led to the large reception hall at the front of the building. To the left as she entered was a room which, if she remembered correctly, was used by the porters as their sitting-room. And one of these porters had been a Lancashire man, taken to the hotel by her father who had employed the man in England, getting his services for the most paltry wage imaginable. But the man had been glad of a home, being quite alone in the world and also being on the wrong side of fifty. Was he still here? Keri wondered. She had felt so sorry for him—Her thoughts were cut abruptly as she heard the voice of the very man himself. And as her name was mentioned she stopped automatically, in the passageway, outside the door of the porters' room.

'She was a rum little lass—full of mischief, and she got the master so riled—by the master I means Mr Paul, not 'is father.'

'What do you mean—she was a rum little lass?' This voice had an altogether different accent and Keri surmised that its owner was Swiss.

'She were always up to summat what she shouldna

be up to. Unladylike, she was. Used ter slide down them there banister rails and land right in main 'all. Plop! It didna matter a toss if guests were there; she'd do it just the same.'

'She sounds a bit of a problem. The boss won't put up with any tricks, though.'

'Not 'im! 'Ad enough with 'er father. My, but they did used ter quarrel. But the master knew 'ow to 'andle 'im and it'll be the same with the lass. She'll have to toe line, you'll see!'

'She should be here about now, shouldn't she?'

'That's right, any time now.'

'What was she like to look at?'

'Pretty little lass—pretty as a picture. Dark curls, she 'ad, fallin' right down 'er back. Expect she 'as it straight now, like the young 'uns want it. And she 'ad the biggest eyes I ever saw! My....' There was a pause and Keri could imagine the old man staring thoughtfully into space. He had often done that, she recalled. 'Lovely grey eyes—colour of Mr Paul's, but whereas 'is remind you of granite 'ers are sort of—of dove-like. Aye,' went on the voice reminiscently, 'underneath 'er tomboyish ways she was a gentle little lass; 'er and me got on like an 'ouse on fire when I worked at their 'ome in England. Kind she was, and thoughtful, not a bit like 'er dad.'

'Mr Hartnell took pity on you, you said?'

'No. Never 'ave known 'im to show pity. 'E took me because he got me cheap. I'd been tramping around looking fer work and he was quick ter see that I'd work for practically nowt! Meanest man I ever met, and cruel. Not like Mr Paul what pays me proper money, even now, when I can't work so 'ard as I did.'

'You said that Mr Hartnell decided to leave you here

11

instead of taking you back to England with him. That would be before he setttled here, of course?'

'Aye, it was. Fer some reason he suddenly decided 'e didna need me services any more and so 'e brought me 'ere to work as porter and general 'andyman. "Don't give him any more than a quid a week and 'is keep," says Mr 'Artnell to Mr Paul's dad. But as soon as Mr Paul takes over 'e ups and not only gives me a big rise but 'e pays me a lump sum to make up fer all the wages I didna 'ave before. Young Keri's dad 'ud turn in 'is grave if 'e knowed!'

'Tell me some more about the new mistress we're having.'

Keri, standing in the passageway, stirred impatiently, her feelings mixed. She hated listening, but on the other hand she was learning something about her partner. But if she had known what was to come next she would most certainly have made a move!

'Well, the best was when 'er kept on doing things she shouldna 'ave. One day Mr Paul comes along just as she lands down that there banister. He says to 'er— in that Hoxford accent what he speaks like— "What do you think you're doing, young miss?" And she, pert-like, looks up at 'im—you know as 'ow very tall he 'is and she just a mite, as it were——'

'Yes, Bill, but carry on with the story.'

'She looks up at 'im and, not a button afeared of 'is ferocious countenance, says to 'im, "I'm sliding down the banisters. What did it look like?" And 'is face gets even grimmer—and 'e was only twenty, mind—and 'e tells 'er in that 'aughty way that 'e so often 'as with 'im, that 'e ain't 'aving that sort of behaviour in the 'otel, and she in turn asks 'im what 'arm she's doing. "No harm at all," says Mr Paul, still 'aughty with 'er.

"But you hare lowering the dignity of this hotel and I ham not having it! Don't let me catch you sliding down them there—Don't let me see you sliding down those banisters again." Well, she was a rare little caution, was young Keri 'Artnell, in spite of 'er dad's domineering ways—'as some of 'er mam's spirit in 'er, I reckon——'

'Bill, do get on with it! I've to be on duty in five minutes!'

'Well, to cut a long story short, Mr Paul catches 'er again. She speeded down that there rail at fifty miles an hour, I reckon, and lands at bottom just as 'e was passing. Wham! They both went spinning across 'all. But next thing I see was 'im grabbing 'er—and in such a ferocious temper, 'e was! And did 'e warm 'er backside!' The old man paused reflectively and Keri, squirming at the memory, felt the hot blood rush to her face. 'My, but 'e did warm 'er! She screamed and screamed, and lucky it was that all guests were out on trips that day. I felt sorry fer lass, but 'er did need a lesson, fer she was a wild little thing. She comes ter me a-weeping and rubbing herself. I reckon she's remembered that belting to this very day.'

The other man was laughing heartily and Keri's small fists clenched.

'It looks as if the boss is in for some trouble.'

'Not 'im. As I've said, 'e managed 'er dad and 'e'll manage 'er. But 'appen she's changed by now. Ten 'ears is a long time. It'll be nice to see lass again,' the old man was adding as, having heard rather more than enough, Keri passed on.

A couple of minutes later she was in the great hall of the castle, glancing round as memory returned. The tapestries and the suits of armour, the heavy oaken chests and the vast open fireplace along one wall. Plants grew in pots—tall palms and bougainvillaeas and other exotic flowers. This hotel had been listed as one of the most attractive—and expensive!—hotels in Switzerland. Luxury was in evidence everywhere, from the deep-pile carpet and richly embroidered velvet curtains, to the smart blue and gold uniform of the porter who was at the entrance, talking to the taxi-driver. After taking a glance to see that he had brought everything in, she went over and paid the driver. Then she made for the desk. A man smiled and gave her an enquiring look.

'Your name, madam?'

'Miss Hartnell.'

'Miss—— Oh!' He stared, examining her face, and it seemed to Keri that he became faintly uneasy, but if so he recovered at once, and his smile deepened. 'Welcome to the Schloss Raimegen. If you will have a seat I'll get Herr von Hasler here in a moment or two.'

'Thank you.' Keri sat down, her eyes on the man as he lifted the telephone receiver.

'Herr von Hasler lives in a chalet in the hotel grounds,' he informed her on replacing the receiver. 'He's coming over at once.'

'Thank you,' said Keri again. She knew instinctively that the beautiful chalet she had seen was the home of Paul. She would have one built, she decided, but it would be right at the other side of the castle grounds!

She rose on seeing the tall slender man approaching across a wide lawn. He entered the hall by the french window she had been looking through and Keri gave a small gasp. She hadn't remembered anyone as handsome as this! Maturity had certainly added a classical quality to his hard stern features, and it had changed the dark hair at his temples to the most attractive

14

shade of iron-grey. Just sprinklings, but adding to that air of consequence and distinction which the man carried so well. His clear smooth skin was bronzed and shining; his grey eyes, sweeping over her from head to foot as he came with a deceptively lazy stride towards her, were, as Bill had said, like granite—and cold as the snow-clad mountains out there.

'Miss Hartnell.' His voice was cultured; he spoke in perfect English as did so many of the Swiss people. 'I hope you had a good journey?'

'Yes, thank you.' In spite of her assurance she found herself disturbed by this magnificent personage who was now her partner in business. 'I hope I haven't brought you from your—er—afternoon rest?'

Faintly he smiled, his eyes wandering over her again. She found herself blushing ... and his smile deepened. Yet his stare held no amusement; it was lazy, yet examining, casual yet deeply penetrating. It seemed to Keri that he was making an assessment of her personality. And with this idea came the astonishing impression that he was trying to decide whether or not he had made a correct decision! But how strange that she should be receiving an impression like this. What decision could he have made? Certainly it had nothing to do with her being here, since he had no control over this. As an equal partner in the business, she was within her rights to come, and to take up residence in the castle. She would want some land, shortly, on which to build her chalet. Also, she might, once she became established here, decide that some changes or further improvements were necessary. However, for the present she would be content to take things quietly, until she got her bearings, as it were.

'I do not require an afternoon rest,' he said at length,

but added, 'you, however, will perhaps like to relax in your room for a while. We can talk later—over the dinner-table.'

Keri looked up at him, feeling uneasy at this rather abrupt way of dismissing her before they had even got to know one another. But she could find no excuse for opposing his suggestion. In any case, she was vitally aware of his overwhelming personality, convinced that any argument on her part would be dealt with promptly, and in a way that suited Paul von Hasler regardless of whether it suited her or not. Of a surety he was a man with an imperious will, a man whose very bearing bore the attributes of mastery and arrogance. At this moment his eyes were hard and merciless and it was difficult to associate this with what Bill had said regarding the generous rise in wages and the payment of monies which should have come to the old man earlier.

Keri's eyes wandered over his figure. Vitality and great strength were manifested in his slender, sinewed build. Nobility was apparent in the set of his broad square shoulders. His half-smile appeared; she noted the even teeth, white and healthy. The man was the model of masculine perfection, she owned, wishing she had had some warning, or premonition, of what she was to confront. For although she had known that the man could display mastery and temper, she had quite naturally concluded that, her father being the bully that he was, Paul von Hasler had been forced to knuckle under to a stronger will. Even the conversation she had overheard, out there in the passageway, had not convinced her that Paul had really stood up to her father. Well, he obviously had stood up to him—and to Keri's mind that was an achievement which only the

16

strongest will could bring into effect. He was speaking now, telling her that she would be shown at once to her room.

'Dinner is at eight,' he added. 'I make a practice of dining with the guests on two evenings a week. I dine with them this evening, so you will join me in the restaurant at eight.' Friendly enough tones, but curt and abrupt. Keri nodded and glanced towards the porter. 'He will take you up,' Paul said, adding that he hoped she would be happy with the room that had been given to her.

'I should think I'll be satisfied with it,' she smiled.

'If you're not then you can change it, but you might have to wait a while, until another is vacant. We're fully booked for the next few months, I'm afraid.' He gazed at her for another measuring instant before, beckoning to the porter, he told him to take Keri up to her room. The porter already had the key in his hand, having been given it by the man at the desk whose name, Keri later learned, was Ernst von Gerber.

The room was large and its view was to the beautiful valley of the Lütchine and away to the mighty snow-clad mountains of the Jungfrau group. Keri breathed a contented sigh and smilingly thanked the porter when, after two journeys, he had brought up all her luggage.

Her flat had been given up and its contents sold, but Keri had a few possessions in the way of books, pictures and ornaments and after taking a quick shower and getting into a housecoat she set about making her room look something like home. True, it was essentially a bedroom, but there was a low couch against one wall and a big cane chair over by the window. The window, wide and very high, opened out to the balcony; this

17

looked immediately on to the grounds and from it could be seen the chalet which Keri had so admired. She must take a closer look, she decided as she began to unpack her things.

Her whole being was flooded with pleasure. To have been poor for so long, and now to have the money for any luxury she might desire, was almost too much for her. She wanted to step out on to the balcony and sing to those mountains over there!

But of course she did no such thing. Instead, she concentrated on what she was doing and when at last she had everything where she wanted it to be she stood in the middle of the room and looked with satisfied eyes at its changed appearance.

And it wasn't only the room that made her happy. In the huge wardrobe hung many expensive dresses and suits; on the shelves were hand-knitted sweaters and blouses from all the best London shops. In the drawers were numerous items of dainty underwear, and on the dressing-table lay a silver brush and comb set, her latest acquisition ... and extravagance! Once again she marvelled that her father had not made a will disinheriting her. She felt convinced that it was an oversight that he had not done so. The very fact of making a will was to some people abhorrent and they often delayed the unpleasant task. Keri recalled that her father hated to talk about death, and she was now certain that, because of his aversion, he had put off making his will until it was too late. Perhaps even at the end he would have done so, but he'd had no warning at all of the stroke that, depriving him of consciousness four days before the fatal result, had robbed him of any last-minute opportunity of leaving his money away from his daughter.

So much on her mind was this business of the will that she actually found herself mentioning it to Paul as they sat opposite one another in the high arched dining-room which had once constituted part of the great banqueting hall of the castle in the days when it was a private residence. She had noticed many eyes upon her as she had entered through the door at the very end of the room. She wore an Edwardian-style evening dress with a long flowing skirt and full sleeves. Her hair, very dark brown and still curly in spite of what Bill had said, came over one shoulder like a soft tender mantle that contrasted enchantingly with her pale skin and the hint of added colour on her lips. She knew without being immodest that she had never looked more attractive than she did this evening. But then her step had never been so light nor her eyes so brightly glowing. Life was good all at once, and her happiness gave her an added beauty, as happiness always does.

Paul's eyes lighted on her as she approached the table at which he sat, immaculate in black and white, the collar and cuffs of his shirt contrasting startlingly with the deep bronze of his skin. His eyes had remained on her, taking in every single detail of her face and her figure. She thought she detected a hint of approval —and satisfaction—appear on his face. But as it was only a fleeting impression Keri could not be sure that she really had seen this particular expression. He had stood up and taken out her chair before the waiter could do so. Keri sat down, feeling rather like a queen!

And it was after the first course that she began to talk about the will—or rather, the absence of a will.

'I still can't quite believe it,' she told him seriously.

19

'You see, he never had any time for me and naturally I thought he'd leave everything to charity.'

Paul was strangely silent for a space before he asked, looking curiously at her,

'What made you think it would be charity he'd leave it to? After all—and I know you won't mind my saying this—your father was the very last person to worry about charity.'

She gave a slight grimace.

'I agree. He was so very mean——' She stopped and shrugged. 'I don't like talking about him like that, even though we were so far apart that we might not have been related at all.' She hesitated as the waiter appeared, to serve the next course. 'I suppose I had charity in mind simply because there was no one else that he could leave his money to—and of course his share in the business,' she thought to add.

Paul spoke to the waiter and for a moment nothing was said in response to Keri's words. When at last Paul did speak his voice was totally without expression.

'Well, as your father didn't leave his wealth to charity, or to anyone else, you can settle down to enjoying it. You'll never need to work for the rest of your life.'

'That is something I want to discuss with you, Mr —er—Herr von Hasler——' She stopped, then added shyly, 'Is it all right to call you Paul?'

He nodded, faintly amused.

'Your father always did,' he said, 'and now you've taken his place.'

'My name's Keri,' she told him, feeling rather foolish because he knew very well what her name was.

'You're telling me to address you as Keri?'

'It sounds better than Miss Hartnell.'

20

'I agree.' A small pause and then, enquiringly, 'You were about to say that there was something you wished to discuss with me?'

'It's about my position here. You obviously work, and I am sure my father worked too. I would like to do some work, if I may?'

'There really isn't any need.'

'I know. But one can't just live an idle life, not at my age.'

'At your age,' he murmured, picking up his fish knife and looking rather absently at it. 'How old are you, Keri?'

'Twenty-two.'

'So you were about twelve . . .?'

She coloured painfully.

'Don't remind me of it,' she begged, amazed that she felt no anger against him for his subtle reference to her humiliating experience.

'No, I shouldn't have. And yet,' he went on in tones edged with amusement, 'I believe it did you good.'

Keri lowered her head, picking up her knife and fork and toying with her fish for a moment.

'I expect it did,' she agreed at last when, it seemed, Paul would remain questioningly silent until she had made some comment. 'Father said I deserved it.' He had in fact declared that she deserved much more, but Keri naturally refrained from mentioning this.

'Your father was a strange man.' Paul stopped to nod to an aged lady who had made a late appearance. 'Have you had a good day, Mrs Craig-Westbourne?' he enquired politely.

'It was wonderful, Mr Hasler. Do you know, I didn't feel a bit light-headed or lethargic up there, on the Jungfraujoch. One young woman was right out long

21

before we reached the top. She had to be left on the train! Now what do you think of my stamina against that? I'm eighty-four, you know.'

He smiled in some amusement.

'Yes, Mrs Craig-Westbourne, I do know. You have mentioned your age once before.'

'Once?' She wagged a bony finger at him. 'Now you're being polite, and as diplomatic as only a Swiss hotelier can be. You know very well that I'm always mentioning my age!'

He laughed; Keri's eyes took on an odd expression as she watched him. How very charming he was now— and yet the severe lines of his features were still most strongly in evidence.

'You are wonderful for your age,' he said. 'I hope I'm as fit at eighty-four.' He returned his attention to Keri as the waiter came over to the old lady's table. 'I was saying,' he resumed, 'that your father was a strange man. I was amazed that he would leave his young daughter to fend for herself the way he did.'

'We had nothing in common. He hated my mother and he said I was like her.'

Paul nodded his head.

'Your father sometimes talked a lot to me——'

'He did? You surprise me.'

'He was a lonely man, Keri—although there was no doubt that he deserved to be.'

'Lonely?' Keri shook her head in an automatic kind of way. 'He never struck me as lonely. He seemed to live for making money. It was his sole object in life. Even before he came to live here permanently he was scarcely ever in England. He was here most of the time.'

'That's true. He and my father managed to get along

22

fairly well together. But then——' He stopped and Keri finished for him,

'You and he *didn't* get along?'

Paul hesitated, his low brow furrowed in thought.

'I wouldn't say that altogether. We certainly had our quarrels—and often! But we understood one another and that was a great help. Had we not understood one another the partnership would have had to be dissolved; that would have been inevitable.'

'He was dreadfully difficult?' Keri finished her last mouthful of fish and leant back in her chair.

'Dreadfully,' he owned with a hint of grim humour. 'There were times when I feared my temper would get the better of me.'

Reflecting on what she had overheard in the passage Keri said,

'You managed him, though, didn't you?'

'He wouldn't have liked to hear words like those, Keri.'

'But you did manage him?'

'I did,' briefly and with an air of satisfaction.

They had digressed, several times, and Keri reverted to the question of her doing some work.

'I'd feel much happier if I had a job to do,' she smiled. 'You'll find me one, won't you?'

'Perhaps, if you insist. What would you like to do?'

'I haven't really thought about the actual job,' she hesitated a moment, listening to the strains of a waltz coming from the dais at the far end of the restaurant where four musicians were quietly playing. 'I thought that perhaps I could help in the management of the business? There must be a great deal of work involved —with all the other hotels as well?'

A silence fell; she knew instinctively that Paul had

hoped that the entire management of the business would be left to him now that Keri's father was no longer there to interfere.

'A great deal of experience is necessary for the management of this kind of business,' he said at last. 'You haven't any experience at all, Keri.'

'Then I shall learn,' she responded firmly.

'I'd rather you left that side of it to me.' His voice was tinged with inflexibility; Keri was riled by it, but she maintained a diplomatic silence. She would bide her time, she decided, and then assert herself. For after all, the business was half hers, so why shouldn't she have a say in the running of it?

CHAPTER TWO

WHEN the meal was over Keri and Paul retired to the lounge for coffee. They sank into deep luxurious arm-chairs on either side of one of the exquisitely-carved tables that were scattered all over the massive room. Chandeliers sparkled above, and through a high wide arch could be seen the glittering bar with its coloured lights and bottles of every shape and size and its gleaming tankards and glasses. Keri glimpsed a tall, elegant young woman with a tray. She was getting drinks from the man behind the bar.

A few moments later Paul was introducing her to Keri.

'My partner,' Paul said with a smile. 'Miss Hartnell,

whom we were expecting, of course. Keri, Miss Curbishly. We call her Gena,' he added, still smiling. The
two girls looked at one another ... and Keri had the
startling premonition that this girl with the hostile eyes
was to play a most important part in her life from now
on.

'You want coffee and liqueurs?' she asked, transfer-
ring her gaze to Paul. He nodded but turned to Keri.
'You'll have a liqueur with your coffee?'

'Yes, please.' Something had happened to the lovely
evening. Keri's light spirit was tinged with the faintest
shadow. She admitted that it was quite absurd, but she
disliked this Gena Curbishly on sight ... and she knew
that the dislike was mutual.

'Miss Curbishly's employed here regularly, I take it?'
Keri was not surprised that Paul should look askance at
her, for her question must naturally have surprised him.

'But of course. She's been with us for about a year
now.'

'She works in the bar all the time?'

'She makes herself generally useful. Sometimes she's
in the bar, or serving coffee after dinner; at other
times she's relieving in the reception desk. She was a
private secretary before she came here; she is also an
expert book-keeper and she speaks four languages flu-
ently. Gena's about the most efficient person in the
hotel.' Paul was leaning back in his chair, one leg
crossed over the other, his hand gripping an ankle.
There was a sort of languid grace about him, and a faint
aura of boredom. And yet, paradoxically, his eyes were
alert as they scanned the room and its occupants—people who had already come in from the restaurant, and
those who were now drifting in in ones and twos, chatting together. He was obviously on the look-out for

anything that might not be quite right, but he found nothing. A young trainee was helping Gena with the coffee, and no one had to wait for service. Watching Paul, Keri could well imagine his being a stickler for efficiency and it augured ill for any employee of his who might be foolish enough to forget it, even for one moment.

The coffee and liqueurs were brought on a tray by Gena; she put them on the table, hesitated for one fleeting moment, and then went away. Keri later saw her talking to Ernst; they had their heads together and now and then one or other of them would glance over to where Paul and Keri were sitting. Keri stared at them, puzzled, and with her nerves quivering, as if she were on the edge of some frightening precipice. How ridiculous! she told herself angrily. She was being childishly fanciful over the wretched girl. She did not like her and knew she never would, but here the matter ended.... No, it was no use trying to reassure herself. There was something almost evil about Gena Curbishly and some inner warning told Keri to be very much on her guard in any relationship she might have with the girl.

'How is the coffee?' Paul spoke conversationally, bringing Keri away from her uneasy musings, for which she was more than a little grateful.

'Lovely, thank you.' She smiled and added, 'What do you usually do at night—after dinner, I mean?'

'Life varies,' he told her. 'We have a dance here twice a week, and then we have firework displays and folk dancing. For myself, I prefer to retire to my own place and read, or listen to records. There are plenty of entertainments in town, though, if that is what you want. There are concerts and shows at the Kursaal.'

26

Keri shook her head.

'I like it here, where it's quiet. I seem to remember that there are some lovely walks?'

'Indeed yes, up through the woods out there.'

'The woods join the castle grounds, if I remember correctly?'

'That's right. I often take a long tramp, climbing into the higher places. The flowers are very beautiful just now.' He paused, but Keri said nothing. 'Here at the hotel we have two swimming pools, tennis courts and putting greens. There are plenty of sources of recreation, you'll find.'

'I shall use the swimming pools,' she said. And, after a small hesitation, 'You mentioned your own place? Is it the lovely white chalet I saw in the grounds here?'

He nodded.

'Would you care to see it, Keri?' he invited, noting that she had finished her coffee.

Her eyes lit up.

'I'd love to!' she exclaimed eagerly. 'It looked so very attractive and I wondered who lived there. I thought that I might like to have a chalet built sometime.'

Paul made no immediate answer to this, and when at length he did speak it was to say he would not care for another chalet to be built in the grounds. They were set out beautifully, for the pleasure and benefit of the guests, and to take ground for a chalet and garden would inevitably detract from the aspect of wide open spaces.

Keri was frowning inwardly.

'You had yours built,' she pointed out tentatively. 'You must have had to take some of the gardens?'

'That particular part of the grounds had not been

27

cleared of the natural vegetation at that time. It had run wild for many years—long before your father and my father bought this place. Neither of them bothered with it; it was left as a sort of playground for the children of the guests. When I made the large play garden you will see tomorrow, in the daylight, I decided to take over that rough land and have a chalet built where I could get a little privacy—have a life of my own away from the hotel and the guests. It's a great improvement on what it was, but as there doesn't happen to be another plot similar, I think you should drop the idea of having a chalet—at least, in the castle grounds. There's nothing to prevent you from buying a piece of land elsewhere and having a chalet built.'

She was shaking her head, and still frowning to herself.

'I wouldn't want to live away from the hotel,' she said. It seemed, she was swiftly realizing, that she was not to be given either the opportunity of working or of having her own real home. Paul had his home, and he had his work. If they were equal partners then it was not an unreasonable attitude on her part to expect the same. Loath as she was—after having met Paul and immediately taking a liking to him—to run against his wishes, Keri foresaw her having to put her foot down, and firmly. How to do this without causing friction was obviously not going to be easy. Nevertheless, she *was* his equal partner and therefore she had equal rights. However, there was time and enough to begin asserting her authority; for the present it was all far too pleasant to spoil, so she refrained from mentioning any more about the type of work she might be able to do, or the chalet she intended to build.

'If you're ready, I am,' she told him when it seemed

28

that he was waiting for her to make the first move.
'Shall I need a coat?'

'It's a warm evening. I don't think you'll require anything extra.' He stood up and she bent to pick up her evening bag which had slipped to the floor. But Paul was before her and their hands touched. For Keri it was like an electric shock—nothing she had ever before experienced. Bewildered, she stared at him as he straightened up. His expression was a mere mask; he, quite plainly, had felt no reaction at all.

'Come,' he said when she did not move, 'we'll go by the side door—over here.' He gestured in the direction of the arch leading to the bar. They passed through it, he stopped a moment to speak to Gena and his smile was swift, spontaneous, Keri thought. And it suddenly struck her that Paul did not smile very much at all. For the most part his features wore that stern set look of austerity that would always remind her of that incident in the past. At twenty he had possessed that particular look; and he still possessed it, but now it was emphasized by the mature lines that had appeared around his eyes and at the sides of his mouth.

Gena's eyes were now fixed on Keri, and there was no mistaking the antagonism that was written in them. Keri shrugged off her misgivings; the girl could not harm her, so why should she be troubled by her undisguised animosity?

The air was cool and fresh as Keri and Paul came out into the gardens. Towering to the sky was the mighty Jungfrau massif, the snow on its flanks and summits azure in the moonlight.

'It's wonderful,' breathed Keri, lightness of spirit swiftly taking possession of her again. 'It's wild, romantic scenery, with, high up there, against the clouds, a

29

wilderness of eternal ice. Just think, the Eiger glacier is half a mile thick!'

Paul slanted her a glance half amused, half surprised.

'You've been reading,' he observed and Keri nodded her head at once.

'Quite naturally I've always been interested in Switzerland—even though I've been here only once, and that on so short a visit.'

'I could never understand why your father didn't send for you later, when he seemed to be so lonely.'

'He really was lonely? Father always seemed so self-sufficient to me.'

'Earlier he was. But for about two years before his death he seemed very lost and alone.'

'I'm ... sorry. I wish I'd known.' Keri's voice was edged with regret. Paul stopped and looked down into her face.

'Don't reproach yourself, Keri,' he said, and it did seem that his voice was inordinately gentle—and so at variance with that severe countenance. 'Your father was entirely to blame. I advised him over and over again to get in touch with you. I know you did write to him at first, but he would not reply. He told me he had no intention of doing so. He was the most obstinate man I have ever known, and he was his own worst enemy,' Paul added with a certain grimness that seemed to betray just how much Paul himself had endured at his hands. Keri thought that Paul must have had to exert all his powers of control not to have quarrelled irreparably with so self-willed a man as her father. He began walking on again and Keri paced along beside him. She wanted to talk about her father, a circumstance that surprised her simply because during the past six years he had gradually become a nebulous figure to her, and not her own flesh and blood at all.

'You were saying that Father talked a great deal to you?' she began, and Paul inclined his head in affirmation.

'Especially during the last year of his life,' he said. 'He was bitter over your mother's action in leaving him.' There was the hint of a question in the words and Keri told him at once that she herself never blamed her mother.

'She must have had a dreadful life with Father,' she added finally.

There was a rather taut silence then before Paul said, his words clipped and almost harsh,

'No mother should leave a baby of eighteen months of age to be looked after by a man. That isn't man's work; he can't do it with any sort of success.'

'I must admit that I always wished that Mother had taken me with her.'

Paul hesitated a moment, but then, after reminding Keri that he had been very much in her father's confidence, he went on to ask if Keri knew anything of the whereabouts of her mother.

'Your father said she went off to America?'

'Yes. She married an American.'

'But you don't know where she is?'

'I've no idea at all.'

'It's very sad.' Paul was talking softly, almost to himself. 'You've had your share of trouble—for a young girl.'

They were approaching the chalet and Keri's eyes were on it. Lights shone from almost every window, and from somewhere under the eaves as well, shedding a soft fairy-tale-like glow on to the lawn and the flower-filled garden. Behind the chalet, forming a stage backcloth like something created by Walt Disney, rose the wild beauty of a world of ice and snow, indescribably overpowering in its gigantic majesty. This was the unsurpassed Alpine scenery of the realm of fantasy; it scarcely seemed real yet its grandeur was almost intoxicatingly impressive. The ragged peaks, towering to the purple starlit sky, glittered in the brittle silver glow of the moon. All was so still and silent, like the hush of a primeval night when total slumber enveloped the world.

Keri felt a strange unfathomable restlessness; she was happy and yet there was within her the sense of a void—an incompleteness that both mystified and disturbed. She did not like it, wished only to throw it off and be quite whole again. She glanced up at the man beside her and swallowed hard, for something seemed to have settled in her throat. Nerves were on edge; senses floundered. She tried to pull herself together, telling herself that the night was so magical that she was bound to be affected in some way by it. These new and exciting surroundings would soon become familiar, and then she would smile at the disturbance of this first encounter.

She was aware that Paul had spoken, said something about her having had her share of trouble, but she did not bother to respond; she was too absorbed in the beauty that prodigal nature had so lavishly spread around her.

'Here we are,' he said as, opening the gate, he stood aside, closing it again when she had passed through.

'Aren't you afraid that some of the guests will become curious and trespass?' she asked.

'There is nearly always someone here.'

'I see. There is someone here now?'

'Not just at this moment, no. I gave Herta—that's

32

my maid-cum-housekeeper—the evening off.'

'I don't expect many people would trespass, though,' said Keri after thinking about it.

'Not the kind of people we get here. They respect the small, unobtrusive "Private" sign that I have at the side of the gate.'

They entered the chalet; it was just as Keri had imagined it, furnished in the modern style but with expensive and aesthetic taste.

'It's charming,' she stated enthusiastically as Paul led her from the hall into the living-room. This was a large apartment with sweeping views from enormous windows covering two walls. The roof was steep over the wide verandah which ran the length of the back of the house. The living-room was at the back and therefore the outlook was away from the hotel and wholly private. The gardens appeared exciting even in the dim light from a misted moon, a light that shone on to the swimming-pool which was some distance beyond the lawn. The water gleamed, and rippled gently, stars reflected on its surface. 'It's not only charming,' Keri amended, 'it's idyllic!' And she was more determined than ever to have a similar chalet built for herself.

Paul smiled at her enthusiasm, clearly pleased. She stared up into his face, marvelling at the inordinate handsomeness of the features. How had he reached the age of thirty without having been caught in the marriage trap? she wondered. Many women must have been attracted by his looks and bearing, to say nothing of his wealth, for Paul's father had left him a fortune, in addition to the hotels and various lucrative properties mentioned once to Keri by her father. Keri's thoughts drifted to Gena Curbishly, although she could see no reason why they should. The girl's intrusion into this most pleasant scene caused a deep frown to appear on Keri's wide forehead, and her companion's brow lifted a fraction in sudden enquiry.

'Something displeases you?' he said at length, when she made no attempt to explain.

'No.' She shook her head, and the frown disappeared. 'It was nothing important.'

'Can I offer you a drink?' He swept a hand as he spoke, indicating the long low couch, at the side of which was a silver-plated lamp standard with the prettiest handmade shade Keri had ever seen. It was of soft peach silk, decorated with pleats and tiny pearls; it shed a soft romantic glow over the place where Keri was to sit. She found herself becoming tensed, wondered what was happening to her that could explain this sudden rapid beating of her heart.

'Thank you, Paul.' Her voice was low and sweet; her grey eyes shone, and for a moment they were held by those harder ones, held strangely and inescapably. Her pulses raced and she knew fear. Fear of what? Keri shook her head as Paul moved away. She was too puzzled by it all, unsure of herself for the first time in her life. But there was something about this man which overwhelmed her, which caused her to feel quite small —and helpless. She sincerely hoped this sensation was not permanent, for there were battles to fight, and in the not too distant future.

Paul, standing by the cocktail cabinet, was asking what she would like to drink. She told him, and a moment later the glass was handed to her. She smiled as she took it; her fingers touched his and once again she felt the stab of an electric shock pass through her. As before Paul gave no sign that he had been in any way affected by the contact; his dark face was mask-like and cold; with a backswitch of thought Keri saw the swift spontaneous smile he had given to Gena.

Almost a fortnight had passed; Keri was still idle—like a guest rather than the partner in ownership, she thought, frowning at the mountains soaring to the sky in front of her. She was sitting on the lawn in front of the hotel, apart from most of the guests who, waiting for the lunch gong to sound, were relaxing in the sunshine.

'I really ought to make my presence felt,' Keri told herself sternly. 'After all, Paul is only a man, not some supreme god who might strike me down should I be foolish enough to incur his displeasure!'

All too easy to talk like this to herself. Twice she had endeavoured to broach the subject of her sharing in the running of the business, but on each occasion she had been stopped by nothing more than a look from Paul. It was altogether ridiculous, and she decided quite firmly, as she rose to go to her room for a wash, that she would have it out with Paul immediately lunch was over.

'Is Herr von Hasler available?' she was enquiring of Ernst an hour and a half later. 'I must speak to him.' Keri glanced up as Gena appeared beside Ernst at the reception desk. She frowned, and the other girl's eyes narrowed to mere slits. No actual animosity had as yet occurred between the two, but without any doubt at all the embers of dislike were smouldering.

'I'm afraid Paul's far too busy to see anyone.' It was Gena who spoke, her voice cold and abrupt almost to the point of rudeness. 'You can leave a message, of course, and I will pass it on to him when I go over to his chalet to take afternoon tea with him.' The beautifully-modelled face was lifted in arrogance; the dark eyes glittered like points of ice shadowed by cloud.

'I wish to see him now!' Anger edged Keri's tone. She wished to make clear her position to this girl who was, after all, a mere employee at the Schloss Raimegen. 'Is he in the hotel, or at his home?'

'He is busy,' murmured Gena, slowly and emphatically. 'You must remember that he is the owner of this place and in consequence his time is fully occupied during the daytime. He might be able to spare you a few moments this evening. I shall ask him when I see him.' The girl would have walked away but, anger flaring, Keri rapped the desk with the flat of her hand, an action which brought a flush of sheer fury to the other girl's cheeks.

'Did I hear you aright?' enquired Keri softly. 'You did say that Paul owns this hotel?'

'I did,' arrogantly and with the most odd intonation in the voice.

'I'm very sure you know otherwise.'

A sudden twist of Gena's lips and then,

'You, Miss Hartnell, are very sure of yourself, aren't you?'

'At this moment, yes, I am. You haven't answered my question.'

Gena opened her mouth, but to Keri's surprise she was prevented from voicing whatever it was she had to say. Ernst spoke swiftly, and in a whisper.

'Be careful, Gena——'and then he stopped, glancing at Keri with a sort of alarmed expression. Keri's eyes widened; it was not difficult to see that these two shared a secret, but how and why should it concern her, Keri could not imagine. Vaguely uneasy, and recalling

36

her initial premonition that Gena Curbishly was to play an important part in her life, Keri walked slowly from the desk, left the main building through the french window in the hall and made her way with the same slow and thoughtful pace, towards the chalet where Paul lived. She rang the bell and the door was opened by a woman of about forty years of age. This, Keri surmised, was Herta.

'Does Herr von Hasler happen to be in?' Keri asked politely and with the trace of a smile. 'If so, I'd like to see him. It's important.'

'Step inside, Miss Hartnell, and I will see if he is busy.'

'Thank you.' Keri watched the woman walk away, towards a door that was closed. This, she thought, was a far different reception from that she had just received from Gena and her friend Ernst von Gerber. Herta had adopted an air of respect, had not dreamed of taking it upon herself to turn Keri away with the summary arrogance shown by that hateful girl who, Keri now suspected, was more interested in Paul as a man than as a mere employer.

'Herr von Hasler will see you,' said Herta on her return. 'Will you come this way, please?'

Paul was at a big desk, his back to the window so that his face was in shadow. But there was no mistaking its sternness, and the slight tightness of impatience that brought his lips into a thin and almost cruel line. Keri frowned to herself, for this was not an opportune moment to approach him, that was for sure. However, she was here now and she meant to have her say, no matter what inconvenience she was causing him.

'Sit down, Keri.' Abrupt the invitation—enough to have put Keri off a few days ago, but not now. Gena and her friend had awakened Keri to a sense of her own authority, and to the fact of her being an equal partner in this business. 'I'm afraid I haven't much time to spare, and it would have suited me better had you chosen another time. However, Herta passed on the message that the matter's important, so you had better let me hear what you have to say.' He looked across at her, his dark eyes flickering, rather indifferently, over her face and that part of her figure which he could see above the desk.

'It's about the business,' she began without preamble. 'If I'm ever to start work then it's time we discussed it. I want to share in the running of the hotel.' She met his gaze squarely, despite the fact that a tinge of angry colour had crept up under the skin at the sides of his mouth.

'I've already pointed out to you that one needs a great deal of knowledge to run a business like this. I have this knowledge, while you have not. Therefore, Keri, I feel we should leave the actual management in my hands.' The former inflexibility entered his voice, and this same inflexibility was there in his eyes, and in the set of his mouth. Keri bit her lip, hesitant about acting in a way that would result in friction between them. Paul had suffered enough of that with her father. True, he had come out on top, but the continual haggling and quarrels must have made life most uncomfortable for him. But after only a moment's thought Keri decided it was better to have an agreement now, a firm and lasting agreement to which she and Paul would adhere.

'As the business is half mine, Paul, I do feel I should be able to run it. I admit I know nothing at present, but I shall learn quickly, if you will be patient with me and help ... ?' She tailed off, silenced by the glint in his eye. A pause ensued, a deep and angry silence that held an almost suffocating quality as far as Keri was concerned. 'I mean it, Paul,' she managed at length. 'In fact, I'm intending to insist.'

That last word seemed to incense him, for his thin nostrils flared. The colour rose higher in his face and the hand resting on the desk closed.

'I'm not allowing you to interfere in the management,' he told her at last. 'I had quite sufficient of that with your father, and I had decided long ago that, on his retirement or death, I should brook no further interference in the way I choose to handle the affairs.' He stopped a moment and looked directly into her anger-flushed face. 'If you have any faults to find, or any complaints whatsoever, then I suggest you consult a lawyer and let him, and my own lawyer, settle the matter for us.' And with that he picked up the pen he had been using and began to write, bending his head so that only the top of it was now revealed to her.

'You promised to find me a job,' she reminded him, her voice trembling with wrath. 'I intend to work, Paul——'

'We will discuss a suitable job later,' he interrupted harshly. 'I'm far too busy now to waste time on so trivial a matter.'

'Trivial?' Keri stared at him. 'I haven't come here to lead an idle life for the rest of my days! I want to know—*now*—just what sort of a job you have to offer me!'

She could have wept at this turn of events. There was now animosity between them, and there would be more, for she fully intended seeing a lawyer, as he had recommended, not only about the possibility of her

39

sharing in the management, but she also wanted to know how she stood regarding the building of a chalet for herself in the hotel grounds. These grounds were extensive, as she had learned on strolling round them the day after her arrival, and she saw no reason why she should not be allowed to take a small plot of land for herself—just as Paul had done.

Paul was regarding her with a sort of quiet anger that was by far more disconcerting than any outburst of fury could have been. He said, very softly, yet with a distinct edge of danger to his voice,

'We will talk about a job for you at some other time. I am certainly not prepared to do so now. As I've said, I'm extremely busy.' He reached forward and pressed a bell. 'Herta will show you out——'

'Paul, I'm quite determined——'

'Leave me, if you please!'

Keri rose, with more speed than she intended, and turned towards the door just as it was opened by Herta.

A moment later she was walking back across the grounds, and when at length she reached the verandah of the hotel she saw that Gena was at an upstairs window, leaning in a careless manner against the french door that led on to the private balcony of the bedroom. She had obviously been intent on learning just how much time Paul would give to Keri. The eyes of the two girls met, and Gena's sneered before, with a shrug of her elegant shoulders, she withdrew into the room and was lost to Keri's view.

CHAPTER THREE

GLOOM had dropped upon Keri like a mantle from which she was unable to disentangle herself. The job she had was that of accompanying one or other of the guides who took the guests out on the various tours. It was a post that had been specially made for her and therefore she felt it was of no real value. At times she actually felt she was intruding, although both Emma and Luise adopted charming manners towards her, and would in fact quite often leave her to do the talking, breaking in only when Keri forgot to mention something important, or had come to the end of her knowledge about the place they were visiting.

'No, I'm not satisfied with my job,' she had told Paul bluntly when he asked her about it. 'I'm merely an extra—and an unnecessary extra at that. Surely there is some other work I can do, something more useful?'

She had had second thoughts about consulting a lawyer, and had decided against it. Far better to avoid more unpleasantness, to make another attempt at an amicable arrangement, seeing that she and Paul were to be partners for many years to come. As for the idea of building a chalet—that was still of paramount importance to her and she was biding her time, ready to take the opportunity—when it occurred—of consulting Paul once again on the subject.

'There's nothing else at present,' Paul had informed her. 'Later, we might be running more tours and then you can have a party all to yourself.'

'I don't particularly care for taking out the guests.'

Paul had made an impatient exclamation at this.

'It would have been much better,' he said with some asperity, 'if you had agreed to sell out to me. What caused you to change your mind?'

'I should have had to find safe investments. It seemed wiser to leave my money invested here.'

'Finding safe investments wouldn't have been difficult,' he assured her. 'Your bank manager would have helped, had you asked him.' A pause and then, 'Perhaps you'd like to change your mind again, and sell out to me?'

'No,' was Keri's firm and rather short response, 'I would not like to change my mind again.'

'Miss Hartnell, we're ready to go.' The call from Luise brought Keri from her brooding reflections and she went out to the coach where the guests were already comfortably settled.

She talked as the coach sped along, informing her passengers that they were now running alongside the River Lüchine. She was interrupted by someone's wanting to know how the river came to be so turbulent.

'I mean,' continued the man who had put the question, 'where does such a volume of water come from?'

'The river is fed from the Eiger and Monck and Jungfrau Mountains,' explained Keri patiently.

'I see. From the melting snows, of course.'

'Of course.' This from Luise, who glanced rather scathingly at the man.

The coach ran smoothly on, with the river to the left. Detours were made so that the passengers could view certain spectacular scenery, not least of which was the Lauterbrunnen Falls—the bridal veil, which fell down the sheer face of the cliff.

Grindelwald reached, the passengers left the coach

and as Luise was far more knowledgeable about the town it was agreed that Keri should take time off to do some necessary shopping.

'We'll meet you back at the coach at half past four,' Luise said, and Keri nodded in agreement. It was a relief to get away on her own; the chatter of the guests, so often inane, grated on her nerves and she wondered just how long she would be able to continue in this present position.

After strolling along the main street, with its backcloth of the mighty Wetterhorn and the north wall of the Eiger, Keri went into a small café and sat down. She felt rather lost and lonely, and beginning to regret having made the decision that had brought her to Switzerland. At home in England she did at least have a few friends and acquaintances; here she had no one at all. She was quite alone and it would seem that it would remain that way, for Paul had no time for her, other than the odd word now and then, that was. With Gena he adopted a friendly attitude and it was she alone who could draw a smile from him, could bring a softness to the dark, saturnine features which, to Keri, seemed to become more attractive with every encounter. That his personality affected her in some strange unfathomable way she would not deny. She wanted a friendship to develop; yes, she desired more than anything that she and Paul would be friends. It was not to be, and had she been fully occupied with work she felt she could have settled down, even without the friendship she desired. As things were she had time to dwell, morosely for the most part, on the rift that was undoubtedly widening between her partner and herself.

The waitress appeared and after ordering coffee and cakes Keri sat back and looked through the long high window. The great Alpine scene was breathtaking, with the massive outlines of the mountains cutting into the clear blue sky. The magnificent glacier glittered like a million stars and with a backswitch of memory she recalled that Switzerland had over six hundred glaciers.

So absorbed was she by the superlative scenery that she at first only vaguely became aware that a young man was standing by her table, enquiring of the waitress if the empty places were free.

'May I?' he said to Keri on having the permission of the waitress to sit down. 'You don't have friends with you?'

She smiled and shook her head.

'No, I'm on my own.' She glanced again at the scene outside, but then she turned and looked at the man. He spoke perfect English, but she was not sure of his nationality, so fair of skin was he, with light gold hair.

'You holidaying?' He spoke with confidence; she knew at once that he was not trying to pick her up.

'I live here,' she told him. 'I'm——' She hesitated before adding that she was a guide. Somehow, she not only felt incompetent to call herself a guide, but for her, part owner of so many flourishing hotels, the job was inferior. Yet the man, after a slight start of surprise, informed her that he also was a guide, and a courier.

'And you're English?'

'I am,' he laughed, and wryly pulled a lock of his hair. 'People take me for a Norwegian or a Dane.'

'I must admit that I myself took you for a Scandinavian.'

'Have you ordered?' he asked, and when she said she had he lifted a finger for the waitress and gave her his own order.

44

'They make excellent coffee here—but you probably know that already?'

Keri shook her head. She was pleasantly comfortable with the young man already and although she was by nature rather retiring where the opposite sex were concerned, she knew no shyness whatsoever at this present time.

'I'm not an old hand at the game, as I suspect you are?'

'I've been at it for nine years, ever since I came from university.'

So he was about thirty, she reckoned—but he looked much younger than Paul.

'I've not been at it a month yet.'

'Not a month! Where are your people?'

'Taking a look at the town. Another guide is with them.'

He looked surprised.

'You work in twos, then?'

'Not usually. But I'm only a learner, as it were.'

'I see.' He leant back as the waitress came up to the table. Coffee and cakes were put before them and then the girl went away. 'Which company do you work for?'

'I'm at the Schloss Raimegen.'

'Hmm. . . .' He gave a grimace. 'Super place, but a most impossible boss. He's a stickler for perfection, so I'm told.'

Faintly she smiled, looking across at him, into the most vivid blue eyes she had ever seen.

'He is. But how have you heard about him?'

The young man shrugged his shoulders.

'One hears everything, with time,' he said. 'Besides, at one period we used to have our people staying there.'

'Oh, so you're with a company, not an hotel?'

45

'That's right. I work for Brooks—most famous of them all! My job starts in England; I gather the little flock together, herd them on to the train at Victoria, then shepherd them all the way here—or to whatever place they're going. Of course, the air's used more often, but there are still thousands of people who are afraid to fly. They travel by ship and train—or sometimes coach—and I go with them.'

'It must be an interesting life.'

'I like it well enough. I intended to travel and this is the only way I can afford to do it. I consider I'm a lucky man.' He smiled at her before lifting his cup to his mouth. 'Name's Doug. What's yours?'

'Keri.'

'It's nice to know, because we're bound to keep on bumping into one another.'

'We are?' in some surprise. 'Why?'

'It's inevitable. You're a guide and I'm guiding too. The tours all go to the same places: Grindelwald, the Jungfraujoch, the Three Passes—— Oh, the lot!'

'Yes, of course.' She paused, sipping the delicious coffee and eyeing the delectable cakes which oozed with fresh Swiss cream. 'But you see, mine's only a temporary job.'

'It is?' He sent her an interrogating glance. 'Bit of a waste of time, isn't it? I mean, you don't learn this guiding lark in five minutes.' His blue eyes followed hers and he seemed to be waiting for her to take her pick of the cakes.

She frowned inwardly, regretting her confidence. She was unwilling to explain that she was part owner of the Schloss Raimegen, and many other hotels, and so she was left high and dry as regards an answer to his subtle query.

'I expect I shall stay in this job a little while,' she told him at length, and as she then took a cake from the plate he too concentrated on what was left.

'Cream cakes aren't good for the figure, they say—but, boy, they are good for the palate—at least, they're good for mine!'

'And mine,' she laughed. 'I could eat another after this.'

'And why not?' he said gallantly. 'I'll pay!'

She shook her head.

'I couldn't let you do that. They're dreadfully expensive.'

'Who knows that better than I?' he grimaced. 'However, as you are not yet a fully-fledged guide you'll not be receiving much pay. So I insist on paying.'

'Oh, but——'

'No buts.' He laughed, a youthful laugh, a laugh that was happy. 'I always get my own way with females.'

At that her eyebrows shot up.

'Supposing I refuse to allow you to pay?'

'Then I'll never speak to you again!' he declared, and in spite of herself Keri had to laugh.

'All right,' she said, 'I give in.' But she felt guilty all the same, for she was wealthy while he was just an employee.

'Excellent. Then we are friends! Have another of these whoppers! That one, with the cream spilling out of the sides.'

'I've had one similar to that,' she protested. 'You have it.'

'I'm okay with these. Go on, take it.'

She did as he told her and they chatted for the next ten minutes or so before Doug said he must be going.

'My little brood are roaming the streets of Grindelwald and might just get lost,' he laughed. 'See you some time!'

She nodded and said yes, she would see him some time.

'Thank you very much for the coffee and cakes,' she added.

'Don't mention it. 'Bye, Keri—oh, and I forgot to tell you that I like both your name, and you! So long!' And he was gone, a rather stocky young man with a carefree attitude towards life and a generous nature. Keri rather wished there had been an opportunity for him to remain with her a little longer. However, on glancing at her watch she realized that she herself should be moving, as the coach was leaving in fifteen minutes' time.

As it happened it was not very long before she and Doug met again. This time she was strolling along the Höheweg—Interlaken's main street, when he slid alongside her in a car, pulled to a standstill and got out, banging the door but not troubling to lock it.

'Hello, Keri! I knew we'd meet again before the week was out. Where are you off to now?' He carried a briefcase and so she concluded he had business to do.

'Just wandering. The shops fascinate me.'

'Full of goodies, eh?'

A swift smile appeared on her face.

'Where are you going?' she asked, her eyes dropping to the briefcase.

'Only to the bank. Change,' he added briefly.

'You do carry the guests about, don't you?'

'It pays off, my dear, as you'll learn—if you have time that is, before you leave the job. They always make a collection for the guide.'

'Ah, of course. . . .'

'You should stay, you know. It's pretty good, taking it all round.' He looked at her. 'Shall we walk along together?'

'Of course.' The bank was farther along, on the other side of the road, and on reaching it Doug asked her to wait for him.

'That is,' he added as the thought occurred to him, 'if you're able?'

'Yes. I'm not on duty today.'

'Super! Neither am I when I've done this. The babes have a day to themselves. Tomorrow they're going right up there.' He pointed to the beautiful mountain which dominated the town of Interlaken.

'The Jungfraujoch?'

'That's right. Been up yet?'

Keri shook her head.

'It's a treat in store.'

'Don't miss it!' he advised. 'It's magnificent up there —makes you appreciate the powers of nature.'

She eyed him curiously.

'Are you interested in that sort of thing?' They were standing outside the Metropole, a luxurious modern hotel in whose complex of buildings the bank was situated.

'In what?' he asked.

'Natural things.'

'Boy, am I! Those who go about life in ignorance of the beauties of nature want their heads seeing to!' Doug wagged a finger at her. 'And if you're one of them, then I'll have to take you in hand.'

She coloured slightly, but it never occurred to her to take exception to his words. He meant them in the very friendliest of ways.

'I must admit I haven't learnt a great deal about such things as geology,' she told him. 'But as regards flowers and trees and birds—well, I am interested, very.'

'That's a start. I happened to take geology at university—had the brilliant idea of looking for diamonds in Africa, working for a company whose boss's son was a pal of mine. But it all fell through as my mother, a widow, had to give up her job on account of her heart—it went wonky without warning. So I needed to send her money right away, and also I need to be reasonably close in case of emergency. This job's just right. I get home after each tour and stay with her for a day or so.' He shrugged all this off and said that he would not be long in the bank and if she would like to wait they'd go into the hotel and have a coffee.

The lounge of the Metropole was very different from that of the Schloss Raimegen, being ultra-modern in its decor, and yet it had a charm all of its own which Keri found just as attractive as the more 'Victorian Lady' type of atmosphere. As if guessing at her trend of thought Doug grinned as he sat back in his comfortable armchair and remarked that this was totally different from the hotel in which she worked.

She nodded her head.

'It's lovely, though. It hasn't been up long, has it?'

'Three years. When we saw what was happening most of us were appalled. A tall concrete block rearing its ugly head above the stately buildings of the Höheweg! What were the planners thinking about? However, here it is, and a fine piece of workmanship, too. Elegance enough for anyone.'

'I agree,' she said, looking around. 'I like the furnishings, also. Just look at that cluster of chairs, with that massive spray of lights over it.'

'It has something, as you say.' He was looking at her, seeing her in profile. Her hair, falling like a cloak about her shoulders, caught the light and gleamed. It also curled attractively and as he watched she took one thick curl between her fingers and began toying with it. 'I like your hair,' he told her as she turned to face him. 'In fact, I like you altogether.'

Her colour rose and she smiled.

'Thank you, Doug,' she said rather primly, and he laughed.

'Don't worry——Oh, yes, you're anxious! I've seen enough to tell me when a girl's becoming wary. But I'm far too engrossed in my job for any thought of a serious affair——'

'I wasn't——'

'Forgive me then if I made a mistake. I don't really believe I did,' he added, casting her a sideways glance that was half-amused, half-perceptive. 'However, as I was explaining, I don't have time for anything serious, but I do like to make friends. Believe it or not, I have platonic associations in every port!'

So spontaneous and frank he was. Keri laughed and felt safe, and able to revert at once to the easy way she had adopted towards him.

The coffee came and for half an hour or so they talked, Doug telling her quite a lot about himself. Keri, with no intention of admitting who she was, allowed him to go on believing that she was an employee of Paul von Hasler. She did tell him of her life in England, and that she and her father had never got on together. He then asked her about her mother and she told him the truth, seeing that a lie would be out of place, gaining her nothing.

51

'Bad luck,' he frowned, and for a moment he was silent. She saw just how serious he could be if the occasion necessitated it. 'So you don't even remember her?'

Keri sighed and shook her head.

'No, I don't. If only I had a photograph of her it would be nice. I haven't anything belonging to her either. Father destroyed every single thing she left behind. I remember producing a handkerchief once, not knowing that it wasn't mine. It had the initial "P" in the corner, true, but that never struck me as strange. You know how it is, people seem sometimes to get handkerchiefs with initials other than their own.' He nodded but retained a silence and she went on, 'Father suddenly snatched the handkerchief from me and threw it into the fire. It was so pretty, with lace edges. He had recognized it as one of Mother's. . . .' Her voice trailed away and her eyes became pensive. Doug displayed great understanding by saying, rather gently, 'From what you've told me about your father I've gathered that your mother's life was pretty grim. If, Keri, she's happy now, then that's the most important thing, isn't it?' She nodded, but dumbly, listening while he added, 'Happiness is something which we have to seek for. Your mother sought for it, and probably found it.'

Keri swallowed the saliva which had collected on her tongue. It was not often that she dwelt like this on the mother she did not know, but somehow Doug was just the person to be with if she did happen to allow herself to think about what might have been. So quiet when silence was called for, so understanding, and obviously tolerant—more tolerant than Paul who had not hesitated to condemn the mother who had left her baby.

52

'I hope she found it,' Keri murmured at last. 'It would be awful if she had made a second mistake.'

'People rarely do, especially where marriage is concerned. Counting out the people in public life, like the film stars and their kind who meet temptation so very often, you don't very often hear of a second marriage failing.'

She looked at him across the glass-topped table, and presently she managed to produce a smile.

'I shouldn't be making you sad by relating my misfortunes,' she apologized. 'Let's change the subject, shall we?'

'If you wish. Personally, I quite often find myself in the position of father confessor. It must be my saintly countenance which tempts people to confide.' He took a drink and she followed, laughing first and thinking that with his very light hair and clear blue eyes he did appear somewhat saintly. However, the twinkle which entered his eyes was roguish, and altered his whole appearance.

At last Doug looked at his wrist-watch.

'Shall we go?' he asked, and Keri nodded her head. 'If you're feeling that way inclined we could spend the rest of the day together?'

A momentary hesitation on Keri's part and then,

'I'd love it, Doug. You can show me around.'

'Fine. Let's get the car, then.'

Once seated in the car Keri enquired where they were going.

'Your choice,' he told her gallantly. 'Say the word and I shall obey it!'

'Well....' Now that she had the offer of being taken out she was at a loss as to what she must choose. 'I was wondering if we ought to go somewhere where

the trips go, just so that I would learn something useful.'

'An excellent idea. Any notion where your babes
are going tomorrow?'

'It's just an afternoon tour—to Bern.'

'And the day after that?'

'The Country Tour; it takes all day.'

'You must be going somewhere else, then. It doesn't
take all day to do the Emmental Valley. We usually
do Bern at the same time, after lunch, that is.'

She nodded.

'We do that. But we also do the Bern tour for
people who don't want to do the whole day tour.'

Doug was nodding thoughtfully.

'I expect your babes will join mine.'

'You think so?'

'You have to fill the coach, and I've only a small
party this time. We're doing the Country Tour the
day after tomorrow, so I guess you and I will be on
the same coach.' He looked pleased and Keri had to
inform him that she might not be on that particular
trip as there were two other guides, Emma and Luise.'

'Yes, I know them both,' he said, stunning her with
this piece of information.

'You do ...?' Her heart had turned a somersault
and now it was beating far too swiftly. 'You know
them well?'

'Of course. All the guides meet, over and over
again.'

Keri felt that she had gone pale. In her imagination
she could see Doug's amazement on learning from one
or both of the girls that she was a joint owner of the
Schloss Raimegen. She bit her lip, wondering whether
to tell him the truth at once. Somehow, she felt that

the easy relationship would be destroyed if Doug knew who she was. She would ask Emma and Luise to keep quiet. They were good sports and in any case they would do as she asked, since they would naturally be loath to anger her by going against her express wish. Yes, she told herself, reassured, it would be quite all right. Doug could be kept in ignorance of her position at the hotel.

He stopped the car at the Savoy, was gone no longer than five minutes before reappearing, a grin on his goodnatured face

'I almost had a date,' he told her, sliding into the driver's seat. 'No, don't let it worry you. It was a Mrs Davis from Chicago. She's alone and trying her best to find a gigolo. Dripping in diamonds and gold —must be rolling in it, as most of these Americans are who come here. Pity she doesn't succeed; it'd be a cinch for some aspiring youth who wants to make a bit of easy money.'

Keri laughed but made no comment. She settled back in her seat as he started up the car; she was intending to enjoy herself, to forget her discontent with the job and with the attitude of Paul von Hasler. Doug was good company and she considered herself most fortunate in meeting him. He had told her that he would be coming to Wilderswil regularly this season, so she was looking forward to seeing quite a lot of him. Perhaps she would not then feel so despondent about her life, and about the disappointments which she had encountered since coming out here to claim her inheritance.

Doug turned right over the bridge and soon the car was winding up into the rocks, passing through several tunnels cut through the mountainside, and climbing above Lake Thun, climbing into a region of breath-taking scenery where thick vegetation gave evidence of rich soil derived, Doug informed her, from the boulder-clay.

'I don't know what that is,' she had to admit, and he obligingly explained.

'It's rubble really, left by the glaciers when they melt. You know we had a glacial period in our country —that it spread across from the continent we know as North America. It spread right across the Atlantic. Well, when that ice melted it left behind all the ground-up rock debris that had collected inside it over thousands and thousands of years. That, Keri, makes the richest soil imaginable; it's what covers the prairies where so much wheat is grown.'

She looked sideways at him, aware of a strange excitement growing within her.

'I'm thinking that I'm very lucky to have met you,' she said, and to her surprise he gave a short laugh.

'Leave your verdict until later,' he recommended. 'Most people soon become bored with my continued lessons on geomorphology.'

Keri frowned and repeated the word in a questioning way.

'I thought it was geology you had studied,' she then continued. 'The two aren't the same, are they?'

'No, but of course they're related. Geomorphology is the shaping of the land, not the composition of it. Ice, snow, wind and rain all combine to give shape to the landscape. But never mind this just now,' he added swiftly and with a slight frown. 'Let's just look and enjoy what we see. There——' he pointed, momentarily taking his eyes off the road ahead, 'just look at that chalet! How'd you like to live there?'

'It's beautiful! The flowers! I love the way everyone uses window boxes.'

'And geraniums. Such an attractive colour.' His attention was back on the road and for a few minutes there was silence in the car. But presently Doug was talking about the spectacular Beatus Caves where one could have a guided tour through brightly-lit caverns where numerous stalactites had formed the most beautiful scenery.

'We might manage to go one day,' he said, slanting her a smiling glance. 'But by ship, across the lake. It takes longer than by car, but it's worth it. I never tire of taking trips on the lake.' Ships were now sailing its placid waters, which extended for over eleven miles in length and about two and a quarter in width. A vast expanse of water whose origin was due to the glacier which, having cut through the mountains on either side of its path, left, when it melted, a huge hollow— two hollows in fact, since Lake Brienz was also left by this glacier. Lovely chalets stood on the banks, their gardens bright with flowers of every colour imaginable.

Keri, enthralled, wanted nothing more than to sit and admire the beautiful Alpine scene of snow-capped mountains and lush trees which covered the lower slopes. The shining lake, the picturesque chalets with their exquisite carving and gay window boxes, the sun overhead shining from a clear blue sky.... It was heaven, and Keri once again dwelt with wonderment on the good fortune which had so unexpectedly come her way.

Bern, where seven bridges spanned the loop of the River Aare, looked almost as if it were an island, so pronounced was the meander. After parking the car

Doug took her to see the famous clock tower where medieval figures began to play at four minutes to every hour. The rose gardens were next, and then the bear pit where the bears—heraldic animals of the town—sat up for the tit-bits offered them by the fascinated visitors.

The buildings were different from anything Keri had seen before; they breathed dignity in the very uniformity of their style, and the fountains lent further colour to the entrancing scene.

'How about something to eat?' suggested Doug at last. 'I don't know about you, but I'm ready for it.'

'So am I,' she returned, but, troubled slightly, she added, looking at him with clear earnest eyes, 'I must pay my way, Doug.'

He hesitated a moment and then, with a shrug of resignation,

'If you insist——'

'I do,' she broke in. 'I couldn't come again if you refused to let me pay.'

It was amicably agreed and they went into one of the restaurants in an arcade. After a meal of *Milkenpastetchen* and apple fritters they sauntered around the shops for a while before returning to the car.

'Thank you for a lovely time,' Keri said when at last they were entering Wilderswil, having returned by the motorway on the opposite side of the lake. 'Will you let me pay something towards the petrol?'

Firmly he shook his head.

'Nothing doing, Keri,' he told her shortly.

'Next time, then?'

'Perhaps. Just depends where we go.'

She said no more, because she saw that he would only be embarrassed by further argument. In any case, they had reached the road leading to the high wide entrance to the castle and he was allowing the car to slide to a slow stop.

'I'll come right in if you want me to,' he offered.

'No, it's all right. It won't hurt me to walk up the drive.'

'You've walked a long way today,' he grinned. 'Okay, then, if you don't want me to come all the way to the front door. I think I understand.'

She turned in her seat, to send him an interrogating glance. There was something in his tone that set her nerves slightly on edge.

'What do you mean?' she enquired, puzzled.

'Well. . . .' He shrugged, appearing to be reluctant to speak. But eventually he did, mainly because he saw that Keri was decidedly anxious for him to do so. 'Paul von Hasler—he's rather autocratic about his female employees, so I'm told. He doesn't approve of their going off with young men they've met over here.'

'Indeed?' Her hackles were up. 'I haven't heard about this.' Interfere, would he? She would very soon put Herr von Hasler in his place if he tried to run her life!

'It could be gossip, but I don't think so.' Having switched off the engine, Doug leant back in his seat and stretched his legs out more comfortably. 'I expect he believes that, with these English girls who come out here to work for him, he must be careful—to protect them, I mean,' he added with the appearance of his familiar grin. 'Bit of a fusspot, if you ask me. Or perhaps it's just arrogance. You must surely have encountered that?'

'I have,' in a rather tight little voice. 'But, Doug, he isn't going to dictate to me! Take me right to the

59

front entrance, please!'

He glanced at her and grimaced.

'Be it on your own head,' he said, and pressed the starter.

CHAPTER FOUR

PAUL was in the foyer when she entered. His dark eyes swept over her with the sort of arrogant expression that instantly sent her temper soaring. That he had seen the car, and the young man, was obvious. And now, it would appear, he was to say something that would be sure to increase the animosity which was so fast rising up between them, forming a formidable barrier which threatened to cause them both some serious anxiety.

'Where,' he enquired, his granite-like eyes holding hers with—she felt sure—the intention of disconcerting her even before she had time to think, 'have you been all day?'

Her chin lifting, she answered quiveringly,

'Out. Have you any objection?' She had naturally looked towards the reception desk as she entered, and was relieved to find that the relief was there, with neither Ernst nor Gena being anywhere about.

The shade of darkness in Paul's eyes became even heavier as, his voice like ice, he told her not to be impertinent.

'Just answer me,' he added, 'and civilly, if you please.'

60

She lowered her head, not because she felt rebuked, but because of the sudden dart of tears that came absurdly to her eyes. How was it that this disunity hurt so much?

'I've been to Bern,' she told him quietly.

'With whom?'

Steadfastly she made an endeavour to hold her temper in check. This was definitely for her own sake, since she had no wish to spend the remainder of the day unhappily going over this interview and telling herself that she could, with a little diplomacy, have avoided an argument.

'With a guide I met at Grindelwald. His name is Doug.'

'Doug what?'

'I don't know his other name——'

'Yet you spent the day with him?' The straight brows were upraised in censure; Keri looked away, determined not to allow this gesture to rile her, as it was certainly in danger of doing.

'He's quite all right. He's at the Savoy.'

'You met him in Grindelwald, you said? Where in Grindelwald?'

'In a café.'

Again the brows were raised.

'You were alone?'

'That's right.' She felt the colour leaving her face as anger took possession of her. The relief at the desk was, fortunately, occupied with a guest and therefore could not know what was going on. However, Paul moved, towards a window seat, and she followed. 'I don't wish to sit down,' she said, seeing him wave a hand in the direction of the seat. 'I'm going to my room——'

61

'Not yet,' he broke in quietly. 'What were you doing alone in a café in Grindelwald? You were supposed to be accompanying the guests on a guided tour of the town.'

She drew a deep breath and counted ten, silently.

'Luise was with them. I didn't know anything about the town anyway, so I could be of little use as a guide, could I?'

She injected a little hauteur into her voice and Paul's mouth compressed into a thin tight line.

'You were supposed to be undergoing instruction— not lingering, uselessly, in a café.'

Her eyes blazed at this phrasing, and subconsciously she was recalling what Doug had said about Paul being something of an autocrat where his female employees were concerned.

But she was not an employee!

'I considered myself at liberty to take a few minutes off,' she began. 'You must remember, Paul, that I am not merely working for you; I am your partner.' She must be firm, she was telling herself. Yet undoubtedly she was overwhelmed by the personality of this dark forbidding Swiss who carried with him at all times this air of arrogance and distinction.

'You consider yourself at liberty to do as you like?'

'I didn't say so. You're twisting my words.'

'You asked me for a job,' he reminded her, ignoring her forceful comments. 'I gave you one. But obviously you want to do as you like regardless of the work which your job involves. This,' he went on in tones edged with ice, 'does not suit me. Either you do the job or you resign from it altogether.'

Keri looked up at him, and at the coldness in his eyes she felt a terrible chill at her heart. Never had she thought to be so unhappy as this. Yet only a few hours ago, riding in Doug's car, she had been gratefully owning to her good fortune. She had felt happy at that time, happy because she was in the company of someone genial, someone who was warm and friendly and who could laugh a lot. Paul von Hasler, serious all the time, haughty and full of his own sense of power and authority, was of a very different brand. And yet there was something so magnetic about his personality that she had to use all her will-power not to be drawn too close. . . .

She frowned to herself, angry at the admission. He was her partner, just that. She wanted him as a friend as well, nothing more. Impatiently he moved, then asked if she had heard what he had said.

'Certainly I heard. I take it, then, that I'm out of a job again?'

'If you refuse to treat the job as a duty—yes, you are.'

'Duty. . . .' She spoke mechanically, scarely knowing what made her repeat the word.

'All my employees learn early that they have a duty to me, that their work is a duty. Any one of them who fails in his duty is sacked.'

Keri's teeth came together. Her eyes sparkled and her small hands closed as fury enveloped her. It was no use trying to practise control with a man like this! He had to learn that he wasn't a god, perched up high on some unreachable pedestal. He was a man, as she was a woman. He was an equal partner with her in this business, and he should be reminded of this whenever Keri considered it necessary. She reminded him of it now, declaring that she was not out of a job, but that at the same time she was not employed by him.

'You're not in a position to dismiss me. And after some thought I've decided not to be intimidated into giving up the job. I shall go out with the guests just when I feel like it!' Doug was in her mind as she said this little piece. If she were to give up the job she might never see him again. As it was, they expected to meet quite soon, when the two hotels joined in hiring a coach. In fact, she and he would meet the day after tomorrow if she happened to be on the coach. Well, she *would* be on the coach simply because she now had every intention of accompanying whichever guide was taking the party out.

Paul's nostrils flared. She had seen him angry, but never quite as angry as this. Her own anger was high, and she felt she hated him at this moment ... but even now she knew a deep hurt within her.

'I think,' Paul was saying in tones knife-edged and cold, 'that you and I will see our lawyers. Something has to be done, and done quickly, because after those years with your father, I am not willing to have the same disagreements with you!' and without another word he turned on his heel and strode away towards the door. A few seconds later she saw him making for the lovely chalet in which he lived—the chalet that was built in grounds that were half hers!

That there was some mystery had very early come to Keri's mind, but she was unable to say when it had come, or how. The secret shared by Gena and Ernst was concerned with this mystery, vitally concerned. Gena's manner—so arrogant, so vaguely threatening as if she were saying, 'Be careful how you treat me, Miss Hartnell, because I have the power to break you.' Impatient with such absurd imaginings, Keri cast them off, only to have them enter her mind again almost immediately ... and this time they did not seem absurd at all. For surely the girl, if she wanted to keep her job, would be more guarded, more respectful to the person who, if she wished, could insist on her dismissal. And there was no doubt about it, Gena was neither guarded nor respectful. She almost sneered at Keri when, after dinner on the evening following Paul's assertion that he and Keri should consult their lawyers, she asked Gena to bring her a drink. Keri was in the lounge, talking to one of the guests who, having arrived there before her, had already ordered his drink.

'I'll bring it when I have time,' the girl said, and instantly Keri turned on her, telling her to bring the drink at once.

'Kindly remember who I am,' she added, aware that it was by no means the polite or good-mannered thing to do, but at the same time determined to let Gena know that she could not treat her with disrespect and get away with it.

'Who you are?' with raised brows. And it was then that the half-sneer curled the dark girl's lips. 'And who, might I ask, *are* you?'

'Your employer, Miss Curbishly,' snapped Keri, furious now and profoundly aware that those guests who were close enough to hear had ceased their chatter and were interestedly absorbing the scene. 'My drink, if you please!' she added, and after flashing her a malevolent glance Gena turned away.

'Funny woman,' murmured Mr Portman, an elderly bachelor who had been staying at the hotel since Easter. He came every year, from Ohio, and stayed until the winter. 'I can't take to her at all. Don't know why Herr von Hasler keeps her on.'

65

'She's attractive,' returned Keri shortly, already regretting allowing her temper to flare before the guests. 'People like attractive girls to serve them with drinks.'

The man smiled a little faintly, his eyes wandering to the girl who, having stalked away, was now taking the order of someone at the other side of the room.

'Men like to see attractive girls around,' he admitted, but added that he wasn't sure whether or not women did. His eyes moved again and, following their direction, Keri saw that Paul had entered and before he could proceed into the lounge he was intercepted by Gena. 'Reporting you,' observed Mr Portman shrewdly. 'However, you're not worrying, I see. You've no need to, of course, seeing as you're now a partner here.' A small pause and then, 'Your father used to chat to me a lot, when he was here. Never mentioned that he had a daughter. Most surprised, I was, when you turned up.'

Keri scarcely heard, her whole attention being with Paul and the girl to whom he was speaking—or, rather, he was listening to her, and Keri had no doubts at all as to what she was saying. Even without the glances sent in her direction both by Gena and Paul, she would have been sure that Gena was making a complaint, simply because she had expected the girl to do so.

Paul's face was tight with anger when eventually he reached the table where Keri sat, still without the drink she had ordered.

'Keri,' he snapped, 'I want to speak to you! Come along to my office!' More controlled than she herself had been, he spoke softly, so that no one other than Mr Portman and, of course, Keri herself, was able to hear.

Without argument she rose from her chair, excused herself to Mr Portman, and followed Paul to his office, glad to be away from the lounge, and the dark inimical eyes of Gena Curbishly.

'Well?' briefly and icily from Paul as she closed the door after entering his office.

'She's told you a lot of lies, apparently——'

'You don't know what Miss Curbishly has been telling me!'

'Well, you seem to know all about the little scene——'

'Which you created before my guests!'

'Your guests?' she repeated wrathfully. 'Just how long is it going to take you to get it into your head that I am as much concerned in this business as you are! As for that woman—she sneered at me, practically refusing to bring me a drink!'

'Refusing to bring you a drink? Nonsense! That's her job.'

Keri, white and trembling, asked him exactly what Gena had said to him.

'She told me how you had treated her—like a servant, with the utmost rudeness. She was embarrassed before the guests and it might interest you to know that she is feeling most upset about it, so upset that I have allowed her to have tomorrow morning off.' Paul's tones were harsh, his gaze smouldering as he looked down into her pale face.

'She obviously omitted the fact of her having treated me with the utmost rudeness—also before the guests. Mr Portman heard——'

'And several others,' he broke in wrathfully. 'I shall not have it!'

Keri said chokingly,

'Nor shall I have Miss Curbishly humiliating me before other people. Up till now she has avoided actually insulting me——'

'Up till now?' he demanded. 'What do you mean by that?'

'There's no love lost between her and me, Paul.' Her voice was more controlled, and although she was unaware of it herself her lovely eyes were faintly pleading. But Paul, angry and resentful that she had caused a scene in the presence of guests, failed to notice or, if he did notice, it made not the slightest impression upon him. 'But as I said, up till now she's avoided actually being rude to me. However, this time she was rude, telling me to wait for my drink——'

'Naturally you would wait for your drink!' So furious was he that he would not hear her out and therefore failed totally to get the picture as Keri would have given it to him. She felt depressed, flat—and most unhappy. Whatever story he had received from Gena had to his ears held more truth than hers, apparently. But then he had listened to Gena, whereas he refused to allow Keri to give him her side of the story. Well, if he chose to believe Gena then let him. She, Keri, would do battle on her own; she had right on her side; she had the strength of possession, and if Gena was not careful she would find life could be most uncomfortable. This resolve being portrayed in her eyes, Paul asked outright what she was plotting now.

'Plotting?' she repeated, eyeing him with a haughty stare. 'You'd better be more explicit.'

His face fused with angry colour, but she was not afraid. She might not be his equal in physical strength and power, but she was his equal in ownership.

'I asked what you were plotting,' he said between

his teeth. 'Answer me—at once!'

Her head lifted.

'Until you can speak to me with the respect due to me as part owner of this business,' she said with great dignity, 'you and I have nothing to discuss.' She glanced up at him once again, noticing the hard wrathful eyes and the taut jawline, and with an inward sigh of utter dejection she turned and left his office.

It being far too early for her to go to bed, she merely went up for her coat and then went out of the hotel into the grounds. The lights threw their radiance into the gardens and as she passed the window of the bar she saw the dark shape of Gena as she lifted a bottle to pour some of the contents into a glass. The girl turned at that moment and their eyes met. Triumph looked out from Gena's, puzzlement from Keri's. Try as she would, she could find no reason for the girl's attitude towards her.

Wandering through the grounds, Keri mused on that first impression that had come to her, the impression that Gena was to play an important part in her life. And Ernst ... where did he fit into the picture? Keri, half convinced that Gena was interested in Paul as a man and not so much as her employer, could not place Ernst at all. Had he and Gena been more than friends then obviously Gena would not have been interested in Paul.

'But I haven't any real proof that she is interested in Paul,' Keri chided herself. 'Why come to conclusions when I have absolutely nothing at all to go on?'

Coming round the side of the hotel on her way back Keri stopped to glance back at the lighted chalet, her eyes wandering from the ornamental shutters to the fountain in the front garden. How cosy it looked, and yet how elegant. To Keri it was all anyone could have desired, and as she thought about her great wealth she felt a stab of anger and frustration run through her at the idea that she could not have what she desired. She supposed the thing to do would be to approach a builder and discuss her problem with him. First, there would have to be an application for permission to build, and then Paul's permission to take some land——

'He'll never give it! And yet why should he have control? He's built one for himself, and had Father desired to have one while he was alive, I expect that nothing would have prevented him from building. Most certainly he would have exerted his authority, have shown Paul von Hasler that he wasn't the ruling power in the business.' He was now, though, thought Keri, turning away and proceeding towards the back entrance to the hotel, the entrance through which she had passed that first day. It seemed years ago! So much had happened, so many disappointments, so much dissension between Paul and herself. Yes, Paul was the ruling power and she might just as well accept it. But no! Determinedly she thrust away any thought of capitulation. Much as she desired harmony between them, she must in fairness to herself stand up to him.

The following morning the coach arrived promptly at eight-thirty and Keri, having informed Paul that she would be accompanying Emma, half expected him to appear at the last minute and demand that she stay behind. But she began to breathe again when, with the last passenger on, the driver pressed the starter and the coach began to move away from the castle entrance. Looking back as the coach glided along the wide tree-lined drive, Keri caught her breath in appreciation of what she saw—the great stretch of parkland with its magnificent trees, cypresses and chestnuts, junipers and white poplars, and many, many others far too numerous to mention. She should by rights have known the pride of ownership as she took it all in, but there was a dead weight inside her which she felt would remain until the day when she and Paul either parted company finally, or became friends with one another.

Her pensive gaze was now on the lovely rose garden, and then on the section of the grounds given over to botanical rarities. Gleaming in the sunshine, and appearing to lord it over all, was an impressive bronze statue of Baron Stratlach, builder of the fortress and one-time overlord of all the surrounding regions. The features were hard and arrogant, the eyes as merciless as the mountain backcloth of corries and horns and mighty snow-clad peaks cutting into the sky. He had a look of Paul von Hasler, decided Keri when first she had stopped to gaze up at the gleaming bronze countenance ... and she had not changed her opinion in the least.

As Keri had hoped, the coach stopped at the Savoy and picked up Doug's party. They were all waiting outside the hotel and he grinned at Keri as he pretended to shepherd in the elderly ladies of the party.

'Glad we shared,' he said on at last getting in. 'Hello, Emma. Nice to see you again. What have you been doing since last we met?'

The Swiss girl laughed and shrugged her shoulders.

'The same as you,' she returned in her excellent English, but then she lapsed into German and Keri saw the grin appear again on Doug's face.

'She's getting married as soon as the season's fin-

71

ished,' he informed Keri. 'You didn't know?'

Keri shook her head.

'No, she hasn't mentioned it.'

'Shy,' returned Doug, and Emma merely laughed. She had willingly agreed not to say anything that would give Doug even the faintest clue that Keri was anything other than a paid employee of Paul von Hasler, although Emma had expressed some considerable degree of surprise, saying that if she owned so important a share in the Schloss Raimegen she would be wanting everyone to know about it. Keri had merely smiled and to her relief no questions had been asked—no embarrassing questions, that was. Emma had asked if Keri was interested in Doug, advising her not to be, since it was well known that he intended always to care for his mother and that in consequence he had no time for any serious affair of the heart.

Doug was doing the talking, a microphone in front of him. The chatter had ceased and the passengers were intently listening to him. He explained that the rivers Lüchine and Lombach had been responsible for the existence of Interlaken and Keri listened most attentively as he told how, over thousands and thousands of years, the two mighty streams had deposited so much debris and silt that the large lake originally left by the glacier was cut in two and the town of Interlaken sprang up on the land in between.

One or two people asked questions, and a young American girl of about nineteen years of age was exceptionally interested in all that Doug was saying. She was clearly keen on him, endeavouring to hold his attention both by subtle play with her eyes and by assuming this keen interest in all he was saying.

'Yes, you're right,' commented Doug with a grin on

noticing Keri's interest in the girl. 'She's chasing—but it keeps her happy, so I don't trouble to inform her that I'm a confirmed bachelor.'

Keri laughed, but she supposed she felt sorry for the girl. She was here with her elderly aunt, so it couldn't have been that much fun for her.

'They've been doing Britain, and decided to take a package tour to Switzerland. The aunt—Mrs Warren —told me that it was her niece's idea, the girl—Susan —has only to ask and she receives.'

'Her aunt came here only to please the girl?'

'I expect Mrs Warren didn't mind so much. She said that this way it was better than travelling here alone. She enjoys the being carried about, as it were.'

The coach was travelling along the same route taken by Doug, but this time the villages on the lakesides were being described either by Doug himself or Emma, who took over from him as the Castle of Spietz came into view on the opposite side of the lake. Emma told the passengers something about it while Doug sat down beside Keri.

'You're not in on this?' he said curiously, and she shook her head.

'I'm learning still,' she told him.

'It takes time,' he admitted, but she could see that he was puzzled even before he added, 'The season'll be over before you get started.'

Colouring slightly, she fell silent, searching for something that would sound feasible. She half wished she could have confided in him, not only because it would make things easier, but because she was feeling so low that it would be a relief to pour out her troubles to someone sympathetic, as she knew Doug would be.

'Shall we have a little time to ourselves later?' she

asked, and Doug nodded.

'We're returning via Bern as I said we would. The babes will wander off to buy souvenirs and drink coffee. We'll take a walk by the river, if that appeals to you?'

'Of course. It's a beautiful day, so what could be nicer?'

By the time the Bernese Oberland was left behind and the Emmen Valley was being entered Keri was feeling very much brighter, thanks to Doug's cheerfulness and his wit. He teased Emma, and often he would tease one or other of the guests. Susan was plainly trying to monopolize him, but his experience was such that he managed without much effort but with the greatest of tact to keep her at arm's length.

'How about this for a view?' Doug spread a hand, embracing the whole impressive panorama of the valley, with the trees sweeping up its sides and the fields bright with yellow flowers.

'It's beautiful.' Keri, entranced by the dramatic change of scenery—from the mighty peaks of the Oberland to the gentle green of the Emmental—forgot all about her disappointments, and even the castle seemed remote, unreal almost. She was enjoying herself with Doug for company and she refused to think about anything that would mar this day.

The coach entered a narrow road before coming to a stop outside one of the numerous cheese dairies of the Emmen Valley.

'And now,' Doug told the passengers as they made ready to get out, 'you're going to see how the famous Emmental cheese is made.'

'What I want to know,' said Susan, 'is how they get the holes in it.'

'Leave it where the mice can get at it,' from someone at the back of the coach.

Susan, flashing him a scornful glance, turned to Doug and, offering him a brilliant smile, asked him to explain.

He merely gave her a cursory glance and told her to wait until she had got inside the dairy.

The cheese dairy was not at all as Keri had imagined it to be. It was in fact nothing more than an ordinary farmhouse or large chalet, with sheds at the side in which the cheese was made. Throughout the valley this Emmental cheese was made by the farmers. This particular farmer and his wife had thrown open their little factory so that visitors could see just how the process was carried out. They saw the different stages through which the milk passed before at last it came out as huge flat round cheeses each of about one hundred and eighty pounds in weight. The holes were the result of fermentation, which was done in a 'fermentation cellar' where the hot damp atmosphere produced gases which blew out and caused the holes.

'If the cheese is classed as first grade,' Emma said, translating for the farmer, 'it is sold as such. Third grade cheese is re-processed and made into cream cheese.' No cheese was exported unless it was passed by an inspector as perfect.

'So when you buy Swiss cheese,' said Mrs Warren, 'you can be sure that it's perfect?'

'Exactly.'

'Well,' Doug was saying later as he and Keri sat together in a café in Bern, 'have you enjoyed it?'

'It's been a most interesting day.' She looked at him, wishing the day were not nearing its end—that was, as far as she and Doug were concerned. But he surprised

75

her by saying suddenly,

'You look—rather dejected all at once. Can I be of any help?'

'In what way?' she parried, playing for time in which to prepare for the next question.

'I have a feeling, Keri, that you have something on your mind—something that you would like to talk about. I know the rumours going around about that boss of yours, and with anyone like you, a kid fresh from England, he can be somewhat overpowering. If you'd like to get it all off your chest, then come out with me this evening. We'll dine at the Metropole.'

Her hesitation lasted no more than a few seconds.

'All right, Doug. We'll dine at the Metropole.'

'I'll call for you about seven-thirty, then.'

She agreed, deliberately refusing to allow Paul to enter her thoughts. In any case, she did not care a damn if he raised any objection or not. Her life was her own and she was not going to let anyone or anything prevent her from dining out with Doug this evening.

CHAPTER FIVE

TEA was being served in the lounge and as Keri entered the hall of the castle she saw Gena moving about among the guests. It had to be admitted, thought Keri, that the girl did go out of her way to make herself useful, turning her hand to anything that had to be done at any one particular time. It was no wonder that Paul considered he had found a treasure in her.

Ernst called and Keri turned, stopping and looking enquiringly at him.

'You had a pleasant trip, Miss Hartnell?' He spoke quickly and, she thought, a trifle breathlessly.

'Thank you, yes.'

'It was a beautiful day for it,' he commented as she turned to walk away.

'It was.' She looked at him, having gained the impression that he wanted to keep her talking.

'Everyone seems to be happy——' He waved a hand towards a small knot of people who had been on the trip. They were all English and were loitering in the hall, remarking on the pleasure they had derived from the trip. 'But the Country Tour is always a success.' Ernst spoke with the familiar accent, and some words were obviously difficult for him because he would hesitate and become frowningly thoughtful, as if searching for the correct English word to use. She nodded in silent answer to his comment and would have turned away again, but he spoke quickly as before, but merely said something trite. Eyes narrowing, Keri glanced around her, her eyes going instinctively to the wide arched opening that led into the lounge. Gena was at this moment hurrying towards a door which led from the lounge, along a corridor, to the kitchen. She had a tray full of used cups and saucers which she was obviously taking to be washed. Turning, Keri saw that Ernst was also watching Gena and now he smiled at Keri and said apologetically, 'I mustn't keep you, Miss Hartnell; you will be wanting to have your tea.'

'Yes,' she murmured, her eyes on the door through which Gena had disappeared. 'Yes, Ernst, I do feel like

77

a drink.' A pause, and then, 'Miss Curbishly . . . she is on duty, I see.'

'She was, Miss Hartnell, but she is now being relieved by Marianna.'

'I see.' Why, frowned Keri to herself as she mounted the wide stairs which curved off from the hall, had Ernst kept her until Gena had gone off duty? It was plain that for some reason he had not wanted her to come into contact with the girl—but what was that reason? In any case, it was only a temporary delay, because she and Gena would meet again tomorrow morning, if not before. At last Keri shrugged her shoulders, dismissing the matter from her mind. She did not see that either Ernst or Gena could do her any real harm, even though they appeared to have some odd plot afoot.

Once in her room she had a quick wash and changed her dress, then went down to the lounge. Marianna, a pretty fair-haired Swiss girl, smiled at Keri in just the kind of way in which she smiled at Paul—with both friendliness and respect. Keri returned the smile and followed Marianna to the table in the corner which Keri liked more than any other. From her seat here she could see both the lounge and part of the garden outside.

'What would you like, Miss Hartnell?' Marianna, efficient and smart in a black dress with a snow-white lace collar, had her notebook ready.

'Just tea, please, Marianna.'

'You are not hungry—after that long trip!'

'I'm afraid I had something in Bern,' replied Keri with a wry smile. 'A pot of tea only,' she added, and Marianna withdrew immediately.

Within seconds of her departure Keri's nerves

tensed; Paul was striding along outside the window and inevitably he glanced into the room. Keri, close by the window, turned her head away at once, but as she looked towards a french window further along the room she saw him enter and make straight for her table.

'May I sit down?' he asked frigidly.

'Of course.' She lifted her eyes, feeling incredibly small as she noted even yet again just how tall he was. He sat down and she felt a little more comfortable, though not in any way at ease.

'You enjoyed your trip?'

'It was extremely interesting.'

A small silence followed. It seemed to Keri that Paul von Hasler was actually searching for words!

'I haven't had time to see my lawyer yet,' he said presently. 'Have you seen one?'

'I don't know of one. Perhaps you would tell me where I must enquire about such things?' She felt lost and very much alone, and intruding into her mind was the insistent idea that it would all be far simpler if she agreed here and now to sell out to Paul.

'I think it would be advisable if you returned to England, and conducted the business from there. After all, you have a lawyer there who understands everything, since he has managed your father's affairs for several years—at least, that is what I was given to understand?'

She nodded unhappily.

'I don't feel like returning to England at present,' she told him, and he frowned instantly. This had more effect upon her than anything else could have done at this particular moment. Her temper flared. Who was he to tell her to go back to England! And who was he to frown like that, expressing displeasure, just because

79

she would not immediately fall in with his own desires? 'In fact,' she added more forcibly, and at the same time tapping a determined finger on the tablecloth, 'I don't intend returning, either now or at any other time—at least, not until I myself wish to do so. And even then it will be merely for a holiday.'

His mouth compressed. There was something exceedingly repelling about him at this moment.

'So,' he said after a rather awful silence, 'you're intending to remain here to make a nuisance of yourself?'

Her grey eyes flashed fire.

'A nuisance!' she cried. 'Just when have I made a nuisance of myself?'

'Several times. Your trouble is that you're your father's daughter and as such you want all the time to exert your authority. It doesn't appear to dawn on you —as it didn't dawn on him—that we are the experts at this type of business. Trainees come from all over the world to learn our art, the art of catering at its most superlative.'

He paused and she watched with interest his changing expression. The pride in his eyes was produced by the knowledge of his perfection as a hotelier. He was an expert at the business and this meant not only the management, but the manner in which he approached the social side, the attitude which, although cool and courteous, held an underlying friendliness, a welcoming quality which was quite plainly of great appeal to the guests, for they returned year after year to this hotel. And it was one of the few that did not close for the winter. It was the only one in the district that catered for those who wanted a real English Christmas. Families came from England over and over again, staying for about four or five days and declaring that they would continue to come for as long as the hotel catered for them.

Emma had told Keri all this and despite the skirmishes she had with Paul, she could not but admire him for the way he ran the business. And it now struck her that, because of his efficiency, she herself was benefiting. Had he not been so efficient then obviously the income from the hotels would be less great. However, he was doing it for himself mainly, she suspected, and therefore was not intending to be overwhelmed by gratitude.

'I fail to understand your attitude,' she told him at last. 'I am your partner, and yet you deny me so many things. Tell me, am I an *equal* partner?'

Was it imagination or was there the slightest degree of hesitation before he returned the answer,

'You know very well that you are. Your lawyer in England explained everything to you.' It was half statement, half question, and she knew a dart of puzzlement.

'He did explain, yes.'

'I had my own lawyer write to him and provide the whole picture.' His tones were still cold and curt, but he appeared to be in full control of his temper.

She looked at him, and a strange tingling fluttered down her spine. Without any doubt at all there was something she did not understand. She said, aware of a faint access of agitation,

'Did your lawyer need to provide the whole picture? I mean, as there was no will and as I was the sole beneficiary, then it was all perfectly straightforward, surely?'

'Certainly it was straightforward; nevertheless, there had to be some correspondence between your advisers and mine.' There was a finality about his voice that forbade any further questions from her. But there was that in both this finality and in the quietness of his tone that increased her agitation. Once again she felt lost, alone in a strange country, and she wished she had someone in whom she could confide, someone who would proffer some good advice. She said, looking at him across the table,

'Why do you deny me so many things, Paul?'

He seemed to frown, but this time it was not apparent, being merely an impression that she had gained.

'What have I denied you, Keri?'

Her lips quivered and she felt a sudden ache behind her eyes.

'I asked you for a job.' She was in a much softer mood now and her gaze was earnest and pleading. 'Surely I can be better employed than I am now?' Even as she spoke there intruded into her mind the picture of Doug, and the pleasant relationship that was growing up between herself and him. However, her ambition was to help in the running of the hotel and any social activities would go by the board if necessary. Doug was after all a very new acquaintance, and if she were never to see him again she would not shed any tears over it and neither would he.

'What you want is to assist in the management even before you know the smallest thing about it.' Paul lifted a hand to bring Marianna to him. His enquiring glance at Keri was answered by her telling him that she had already ordered and so he just gave his own order to the girl. 'It's impossible,' Paul went on when Marianna had left the table. 'As I said at first, there isn't any need for you to work at all.'

'And I told you that such a situation would be impossible for me. I've never been idle and I don't intend to start now.' A small silence followed, with Paul preoccupied by his own thoughts. 'The other thing you've denied me is the house.'

'House?' He looked uncomprehendingly at her.

'I want to build a chalet for myself.'

Paul shook his head emphatically.

'There is no place that can be used for the building of a chalet.'

'There's plenty of space; you're just making excuses. Why——' She spread a hand towards the window. 'What about all that parkland?'

'You'd spoil it by building on it?'

'I could build somewhere near to yours—oh, not on top of it, as it were, but within reasonable distance. You know very well that to have it built would not interfere with the view at all. No trees would have to be cut down, and there is a tiny stream that could run through the bottom of my garden.' She recalled that at first she decided to build as far as possible from Paul's chalet, but now she would be satisfied with any plot of land he would allow her to have.

'You appear to have done some surveying already?' Cool and short the tones, and his eyes held a glint which she did not like at all.

'I've taken a good look, yes.' She sighed with impatience. 'Paul, I hate to keep on reminding you, but I *am* joint owner of this place—and many other places,' she thought fit to mention. 'I haven't even been taken to see any of them yet.'

'I have intended taking you to see some of the other hotels, but I've been far too busy here. We have managers in all of them and it is of course incumbent on me to take you and introduce you to these managers.

83

You must be patient—for another couple of weeks at least. I shall then have time to take a few days off——'

'A few days?' It was only after she had put the question that she realized just how little she knew about her inheritance. Two hotels were in Lucerne and two in Geneva, but she had no idea where the others were. They had not seemed important; she had been totally absorbed by the Schloss Raimegen; its charm had been with her since she was a child, when she had been brought here by her father. The others seemed not to be important, for it was here she wished to live, in this lovely ancient castle on a hill overlooking the beautiful wooded valley, a valley of dream-like beauty in its own right, but with its backcloth of mighty shimmering peaks it was nothing short of superlative. The frozen world above was dominated by the staggering massif of the Jungfrau group, but many more majestic peaks contributed to the awe-inspiring scene of nature's glory.

'We shall have to make a tour,' Paul was explaining, 'in order to take in all the hotels.' He looked directly at her. 'Ours is a large and important group, Keri. And, in addition, I am negotiating for the purchase of hotels in the Caribbean.'

Her eyes widened. Paul von Hasler was certainly a businessman and no mistake!

'You said *you* are negotiating. Does this mean that I am not in on this prospective deal?'

He inclined his head.

'It does, I'm afraid. I wish to have full control of any new hotels that might be bought.'

'So. . . .' She frowningly considered this piece of information. 'It could mean the break-up of our partnership?' She was bewildered and it showed. 'I don't know much about these things,' she added before he could speak.

'Our partnership must continue while ever you want it to,' he said. 'However, Keri, I would advise you to think over the advice I have given you. I have informed your lawyer in England of the amount I'm willing to pay in order to buy you out——'

'It must be a great sum. You have that sort of money?' The question came involuntarily and she knew as soon as it was uttered that she had made a mistake. Paul's whole manner changed, reverting to the frigid attitude which he had adopted with her a few minutes ago.

'I should hardly be making the offer if I had not the money to pay,' he said tautly. 'Yes, it is a large sum, and as I was about to say when you interrupted me, you will be a very wealthy woman. I'm sure that if you seek the right advice, you will see the sense of my proposition.' He paused, but she made no comment, and he went on to say that if it was investments which worried her he would be only too willing to help her. 'I myself have money invested, and I could advise you about investing yours.' Still she said nothing and as the tea had arrived both he and Keri fell silent as they poured themselves a cup from their own separate teapots.

'Paul,' she said after a long time, 'is there no possibility of our coming to an agreement—without my selling out to you, I mean?'

He studied her face, noting the slight quivering of the lips, the tension portrayed by the movement of a vein in her temple. And quite suddenly his face softened and he said, almost gently,

'You don't want to sell out to me, do you, Keri?'

She gave a deep, quivering sigh, unconsciously, little

realizing just how helpless she appeared to him, this man with such confidence and self-possession. Her face was pale but still very beautiful; her hair framing it was long and silky and shining with cleanness. All this he took in before his glance fell to her hand, toying nervously with the spoon in her saucer. Aware suddenly of his eyes upon her hand, she put the spoon down and dropped her hand to her lap.

'You know I don't want to sell out to you,' was her quiet reply. 'I love it here....' Her voice trailed away as she swallowed, trying to dissolve the lump in her throat. 'This castle ... I feel so privileged to be living in it even though it is now an hotel.' Again she paused, to glance around her, and to appreciate the Renaissance and early Baroque influences which were so important in adding atmosphere to the interior of the castle. 'I know I've said I want a chalet, that's because I do love privacy, which isn't possible here. But it would be at least a year before the chalet was completed and ready to be lived in and meanwhile I should really enjoy being here. After that, were I working, I should be coming every day.' Her pensive eyes returned to his dark face. Its softened aspect was still there and she fluttered him a smile. 'If we could only agree...?'

He seemed a trifle distressed, much to her amazement. He took a drink, his eyes wandering mechanically to the door, when two couples came through it. They sat down and ordered tea, one of the men lifting a hand in salute as he noticed Paul sitting there. An inclination of his head was all the response Paul gave, but it was sufficient to satisfy the man. There was no doubt about it, Paul had a very special way with him; he could be as cool as he liked yet convey friendliness to anyone who sought it.

Returning his eyes to Keri, he said gently,

'You and I shall have dinner together in my home. It will be quiet, private, and we can have a talk about these problems.' He paused and frowned as if in self-admonition. 'Perhaps I haven't been as understanding as I should——' He smiled at her then, a full smile and the most charming she had ever had from him. Her own smile came swiftly and her heart was light even though she had to turn down his offer, saying that she had already made arrangements to go out this evening. Disappointment within her was high, but she was not too troubled as she suggested they have their intimate little dinner and talk on the following night. But Paul shook his head immediately. He was not free, he told her.

'I'm surprised that you're off out this evening,' he went on. 'You've made some friends?'

'It's Doug,' she said, not without some difficulty. Why, she asked herself, hadn't she found out his second name?

'I see. . . .' He shrugged his shoulders and added, 'Well, we shall have to postpone our talk.' He drank up and rose from his chair. 'I'll say goodnight, then, since it's unlikely we shall meet again this evening. I'm going early to my home—having dinner there, as I said.'

She watched his tall figure move with ease and swiftness across the floor. Then he was gone, striding towards his chalet.

Doug called for her at half-past seven as promised and took her to the Metropole. They had drinks first and then Doug told her about the Fondue Restaurant downstairs. It sounded different, and exciting, so Keri agreed to try it.

'Isn't it attractive?' Keri looked all around her, appreciating the thought that had gone into the making of this 'kitchen-like' cellar restaurant. On the walls were hung all kinds of kitchen utensils, all in burnished copper. The furniture was pine, the tables being of the kind used in old-fashioned kitchens, and the chairs the same.

They ordered a meat fondue—it was brought to them in thin slices which they rolled on long sticks and held in the water for a few minutes until cooked. All kinds of sauces and pickles were arrayed round the gleaming copper fondue pan.

'I don't know where to begin,' laughed Keri, amazed at the way she felt, having lost her dejection altogether as soon as she and Doug drove away from the Schloss Raimegen. Dwelling on this change, Keri did begin to consider leaving and returning to England. For it was more than clear that she would be happier in mind if she were free of the influence of Paul von Hasler. And there was also Gena, and Ernst, both of whom acted most strangely at times. Ernst, it was true, treated her with some measure of respect, but he was strange for all that. Gena's attitude was one of supercilious triumph, as if she held in her hand four aces—and knew just when and how to use them.

'What are you thinking about?' Doug, smart in a light blue suit and cream shirt, looked gravely at her; she had noticed with a faint sense of regret that his familiar grin had not appeared once since they sat down over a quarter of an hour ago.

'It's . . . nothing, Doug.'

'The hesitation tells its own tale. Like to talk?'

She took a long strip of meat from her plate and began rolling it round her stick, watching it idly as it got shorter and shorter.

'I suppose I want to talk, really,' she sighed.

'Fire ahead, then. I won't give away any secrets.'

She smiled then and said,

'I have no need to be told that, Doug.'

'Thanks for the trust.' He paused, watching her toy with the meat before dropping it into the water which, by now, was becoming a rich, delicious-smelling stock.

'Is it your boss?'

'Partly.' Keri kept her eyes on the stick she held. 'But partly others.' This came out on its own. She had no regrets, though, because as she had implied, she could trust Doug to keep silent about anything she might decide to tell him.

'The glamorous Miss Gena Curbishly?' suggested Doug, bringing Keri's eyes up in surprise.

'What made you say a thing like that?'

A curve to his lips—almost a sneer, and Keri frowned disbelievingly. She would never have believed that Doug *could* sneer.

'She's notorious for being jealous of anyone whom Paul von Hasler might take a liking to.'

Take a liking to.... Keri said,

'He isn't interested in me—not in that sort of way.'

Doug gave her an appreciative look.

'You're lovely enough to attract even his attention.'

She blushed, as was to be expected, but, retaining her control, she asked what he meant by the 'even his'.

'Well, he doesn't strike one as being over-interested in women, does he?'

'No, I suppose not.' Something touched her senses, and her nerves. Filtering into her consciousness was the inexplicable sensation of a desire unobtainable ... a pleasure out of reach. 'No, he's so aloof, so reserved.

He seems to be a man apart, a man totally self-sufficient.'

Doug was smiling, watching her expression as she spoke.

'You've weighed him up expertly—and it hasn't taken you very long, either.' He paused a moment and then, 'Is it Gena?' he asked again, and she nodded her head immediately. 'What's she been doing to you?'

'She acts as if she has some sort of——' Keri frowned and stopped. 'No, not a hold exactly.' She looked across at him, so preoccupied that she forgot to take out her meat, and it continued to stew on the end of the stick she held. 'She acts as if she knows something about me which could do me harm——' Again she stopped, and her frown deepened. 'That sounds absolutely ridiculous, doesn't it?'

'I must admit that it does. What could she know about you?'

'Nothing that I can think of.' But, having begun to confide, Keri continued, telling him about Ernst and her impression that he and Gena shared a secret. Watching him, she realized that his interest was growing as her story came out, and when she had finished his lips were pursed and his brows drawn together as if in concentration.

'And this afternoon Ernst deliberately kept you away from Gena?'

'I'm sure he did. He could see I wanted to get away, but he kept me talking. I then noticed that he was watching Gena and as he knew she was due to go off duty any moment he watched for her going out. When she went off with a piled-up tray he knew that was her last journey. It was then that he let me go.'

'Seems funny,' he mused. 'He must have known that

you and Gena would meet soon anyway.'

'That's what I thought.'

'It seems, if your impression holds any weight, that it was only at that particular time that he wanted to keep you apart.' He stopped to point out to Keri that her meat would be overdone and with a grimace she brought it out and gingerly put it to her lips. 'Does that sound logical?' enquired Doug, continuing with what he was saying before he interrupted himself.

'It sounds logical, but it's puzzling. I would naturally be going into the room for my tea, but I was going up to my room first.'

'Ernst didn't know that, though. Most people, coming in from a trip, go in to afternoon tea straight away, then go up to their rooms to change for dinner.'

Keri nodded in agreement.

'If your deductions are correct,' she said after rolling another strip of meat around her stick, 'then he must have been *afraid* of our coming into contact with one another at that particular moment.'

'Seems to be the case.' That Doug was becoming more and more puzzled was plain, but Keri was totally unprepared for the blunt question that came next. 'You're keeping something back, aren't you, Keri?' His gaze was intent and it was he now who had forgotten to take out his meat.

She started and went a trifle red. Doug quietly reminded her again that she could trust him implicitly; he also pointed out that if she wanted help and advice from him then she would have to give him the whole picture.

'That, or none at all,' he ended and, after the briefest hesitation, she told him the whole truth, noting the slow widening of his eyes as he learned that she was the partner of Paul von Hasler.

'I didn't tell you at first because it didn't seem to be the thing,' she ended a little haltingly, because of the guilt she felt at deceiving him. 'But you'll understand that, as we were total strangers, it would not have been the right thing for me to do?'

To her utter relief he quickly told her that he certainly did understand.

'As you say, we were strangers, and one does not begin telling a stranger that one is a millionairess——'

'I'm not that,' she broke in. And then, 'Oh, Doug, I'm so glad you're not feeling angry about it. I just could not bring myself to tell you, even later, when we went together to Bern. And today——'

'Don't worry about it,' he broke in reassuringly. 'After all, you were not bound to mention so personal a thing either to me or to anyone else. I'm rather puzzled, though, that neither Emma nor Luise has mentioned it to me.'

Keri bit her lip, and the colour fused her cheeks again.

'I asked them not to mention it, nor to mention my surname, because you'd have immediately associated me with the Mr Hartnell who was Paul's partner.'

'I most certainly would have done. So your name's Hartnell. Mine's Balman. Sorry about the omission.'

'You're not offended by my reticence?'

'Keri, girl, don't look like that! And get on with your eating! I'm not the sort of chap to become offended so easily. As I've said, it was not incumbent on you to divulge your personal affairs to me.'

'Thank you for being so understanding. You've no idea how different I feel now that I've told you everything,' she went on to add, smiling and hoping that they would continue to discuss her problem, so that Doug could help her unravel the mystery. 'My appetite's improved too,' she ended with a laugh.

'Good.' He looked hard at her. 'You know, Keri, you're not at all cut out for the part.'

'The part?'

'Of hotel owner. You know, the "big business" type of woman. You're soft and feminine and—forgive me for this—cut out for the position of adored wife to some lucky man. I can see you with a couple of super kids——'

'Doug—*please!*' She was blushing enchantingly, and her long silky lashes came down, throwing shadows on to her cheeks. Her hair in the candlelight was shining and soft against the clear, peach-bloom skin of her face and neck. 'If we can talk about this mystery . . .?'

'Okay,' he laughed, but added, 'By golly, if I were not so absorbed in my job and my mum . . . Oh, well, never mind. I'll dance at your wedding, though, and if I've any regrets I'll hide them!'

She had to laugh, but at his mention of her wedding her thoughts went automatically to a lean brown face, a face cold and arrogant . . . the face of Paul von Hasler.

Doug began speaking and the picture faded.

'As we've decided, there definitely is a mystery.' He was a different man now, brisk and businesslike, and in answer to her unspoken surprise he confessed that he had a cousin who was a detective. Doug had at one time spent a week with this cousin, when he was engaged on a case of smuggling, and Doug had learned a great deal from him.

'It was darned interesting, I can tell you. And without being immodest I believe I did help a little. So you've picked on the right man to help you unravel

93

your mystery.'

'You really think it can be unravelled?' was her swift and eager query.

'I have such close contacts with those working in the hotel that I should say it might be possible to learn a few things which would help. One thing I learned from my cousin was how to investigate without anyone realizing that you were doing it. Being subtle in your approach; keeping eyes and ears open—yet assuming an attitude of total disinterest. I have an advantage because no one will suspect me of playing the detective.'

'You mean—Gena might talk?'

At this he shook his head.

'She's too smart for that. But I've always got on well with Ernst....' He went on talking for a while and Keri listened, feeling fortunate that she had found someone so reliable and trustworthy. He was efficient too, and she liked the way he kept on stopping to think, as if he were formulating a plan of action. 'This promises to be exciting,' he exclaimed at last. 'Life can become dull at times and a diversion like this is welcome!'

'It's very good of you to help,' she began, when he interrupted her with,

'I'm *offering* to help, Keri. Don't soar away into a cloud of optimism, as women do! You and I have a problem to solve and we shall do our best to solve it, but we can fail, remember.'

She nodded and after a short pause asked him if he thought that Paul's attitude had something to do with the mystery.

'Yes, I do,' he said, but that was all. His opinion was kept to himself and after noting his expression she made no attempt to draw him out. He had a notion, that was plain, but it was not in any advanced stage. When it was, he would tell her about it; of this she was certain.

Their conversation ceased altogether as the waiter appeared at their table.

'You have finished?' he enquired in slightly broken English.

'Yes; it was delicious.' Doug was eyeing the stock, bubbling slightly over the spirit stove which burned beneath it. Keri watched, surprised and fascinated as the waiter, after having poured the stock into the two soup plates he had brought with him, proceeded to break an egg into each. The hot liquid partly cooked the eggs and the plates were put before Doug and Keri.

'Thank you,' was all the waiter said before giving a slight bow and moving silently away from the table. Doug looked at Keri and laughed. 'Obviously you haven't seen anything like this before.'

'I haven't. You'll remember that I told you I'd never had any money to spend on going out to dine.'

He frowned and passed some remark about her father's stupidity.

'But now you can have anything you want,' he ended.

'Within reason.' She thought of the chalet and gave a small sigh. 'I do wish that Paul would relent over the question of the home I want, though.'

'As you say, Keri, you have as much right as he to build a house for yourself.'

'I suppose I should insist.'

'Would it be wise?' He looked at her shrewdly as he added, 'The position's already upsetting you, that's for sure. If you take my advice you won't worsen it by asserting your authority, at least, not yet awhile.'

Keri nodded mechanically.

'We couldn't possibly go on if the situation becomes worse between us. Partners must agree, in the main, that is,' she added quickly, and with a faint smile he returned,

'You were suddenly put in mind of your father, obviously.'

'I was. I can't think how that partnership survived, but it did.'

'And yours could too, were you a man. But you're a girl, and a not very assertive girl at that.'

'I intended to be assertive,' she told him, 'but it doesn't seem to have materialized.'

'It's owing to Herr von Hasler's arrogant and authoritative ways,' was Doug's perceptive rejoinder. 'No female's a match for him when it comes to a battle of this kind; that's why I've advised you to hold your horses for a while, just until we've done something about unravelling the mystery....' His voice trailed away to silence and, turning her head to follow the direction of his gaze, Keri saw Gena and Ernst just coming into the restaurant.

'Our two suspects,' murmured Doug, and then, returning his gaze to Keri, 'It's fortunate that we're well hidden behind this screen, and it's also fortunate that we've finished our meal. Up you get——No, not in a hurry, and keep your face turned that way, towards the far door through which we can leave unseen, if we're careful.'

'It's impossible, Doug!'

'Not at all,' was his mild rejoinder. 'Just rise slowly, and keep this side of that minature forest of plastic greenery. Good girl!'

'Why did you want us to leave without their seeing

us?' Keri was asking a few minutes later as, after making a successful exit from the main dining-room, they had stopped only so that Doug could pay the bill, upsetting the hotel's routine somewhat by this unorthodox manner of leaving the table.

'It's best that they don't see us together,' was all the explanation he offered. 'You didn't tell me that Ernst and Gena had the evening off.'

'I didn't know,' she returned, walking beside him as he made his way to the stairs leading to the ground floor and to the way out.

'It's of no account.' He glanced over his shoulder. 'Bit of luck, that. Had they seen us together it might have hampered my enquiries.' He sounded eager and she was not surprised to hear him say that he wished he could have re-entered the restaurant and deposited himself somewhere where he could listen in to their conversation unseen.

'Is that possible?' she asked, her heart thumping at the thought, so risky did it seem.

'Could be.' They had stopped by the car. 'If they sit on that far side—the same side as the serving counter—then I could sit on that table for one by the wall.'

'The one practically hidden by the potted plants?'

'It would be *completely* hidden by the plants, once I'd finished messing about with them!' He turned to her with an urgent gesture. 'Look, Keri——'

'I know what you're about to say,' she interrupted with the same urgency. 'Doug, if you want to try, then leave me. I can find my way home by taxi.'

'I don't like the idea. . . .' But his eyes strayed to the door of the hotel. 'All right! I'll call a taxi for you——'

'No, don't bother. I'll go into the hotel and get the

97

receptionist to phone for one for me. You go, Doug—and good luck!' She was just as excited as he, although she was still uneasy about the risk. Noticing this by the expression in her eyes, Doug said reassuringly,

'I'll not take any risks. Should there be any chance of my being discovered I shan't even sit down. All right?' She smiled then, and nodded. 'The lord help my stomach!' he exclaimed as he turned with her and they walked back into the front entrance of the hotel.

'The waiter's going to consider you the biggest glutton alive!'

'I'll telephone you some time tomorrow, calling myself Kaspar Stouri. You were enquiring about buying a car from me.'

'Was I?' with a wide and amused stare. 'Is there a real Kaspar Stouri?'

'Hundreds of them, I shouldn't wonder. This particular one's a friend of mine—he's a car dealer in Bern.'

'Ah.... And so anyone taking the call will not be in any way suspicious. I do have a telephone in my room, of course, so no one will be able to overhear.'

'No?' with raised eyebrows. 'Look, Keri, all I shall say to you is that I have a small car which might just suit you. I will then tell you a time that will be convenient for you to call at my garage. But you will not call at any garage, but be at the landing-stage at that time. We'll then go off on a sail on Lake Brienz and talk.'

Having entered the hotel Keri went to the desk while Doug made for the stairs. Having reached them he turned, and Keri saw the familiar grin transform his face.

'By the way,' he called, 'if I don't ring you you'll

know I'm down with gout—that's what you get when you over-eat!'

She laughed, but he was gone.

'Yes, madam, what can I do for you?' The receptionist spoke politely and softly, bringing her round from her contemplation of the place at which Doug had disappeared.

She smiled and said,

'If you would be so kind as to call a taxi for me ...?'

'Certainly, madam,' smiled the man, and picked up the telephone receiver.

CHAPTER SIX

QUITE unexpectedly Keri came face to face with Paul as she entered the hall of the castle. Ignoring her glance of surprise, he asked how she came to be returning in a taxi when she had been out with Doug.

'He has a car,' he stated. 'Why didn't he see you safely back?'

At the arrogance of the tone, the demanding attitude, and the interrogating expression in his eyes, Keri felt her temper rise. But, unwilling to run the risk of sleepless hours brought about as a result of a quarrel with her partner, she spoke quietly, and there was even a placatory note in her voice as she replied,

'I came home by taxi because Doug had some business to attend to—important business.'

'At this time of the night?' With a deliberate flick

of a white cuff Paul glanced at his watch, an action which caused an angry intake of her breath. But still she retained her calm, refusing to be drawn into a quarrel with him.

'He gave me to understand that he had something important to see to.' She lowered her lashes, hiding her expression, just in case it should betray her.

'Sounds most unusual to me,' returned Paul thoughtfully. 'In any case, it was his duty to see you home after taking you out to dinner.'

Again she drew a deep breath, determined not to allow her temper to be frayed by anything Paul said.

'I offered to come back by taxi.' She and Paul were standing by the large glass door and, glancing to one side of him, she glimpsed the magnificent view of the mountains, dramatically outlined in the light of a full moon. Never had she imagined that she would ever be fortunate enough to live with land that was so perfect. She had grown to love the mountain scene of snow-draped heights and glistening cascades falling from them, of lush green lower slopes where clean brown cattle grazed, their bells echoing across the valley. Every moment could have been bliss, she thought, bringing her eyes back to Paul's stern set face. Why was he so austere, so incalculable? She recalled those times when he had softened, had smiled at her and spoken with some measure of understanding. Yes, he could be different if he so desired, exuding the greatest charm possible.

'And he allowed you to do so.' Crisp the tone but with a strange inflection which caused her eyes to flicker with a puzzled light. The fact was that Paul von Hasler appeared to be far too interested in her actions ... disproportionately angry at Doug's having left her to come back to the hotel on her own. Could it be possible that he was anxious about her welfare? The idea sounded absurd to her own mind, and yet it persisted. But presently Paul gave a shrug of his shoulders and, after changing the subject to tell her that there would be no tour taking place on the following day, he bade her a stiff good night and left her, his long legs carrying him swiftly across the lawn as he made for his chalet, the lights of which could be seen twinkling through the branches of the trees. Turning to the stairs, Keri gave a deep sigh, reflecting on Paul's manner earlier on when he had asked her to dine with him in his chalet. She tried to imagine the scene, thinking that he would prefer a candlelit table to having brighter lighting, for even in the restaurant here each table had its own ornate candle, placed in a coloured jar. Paul would also have beautiful silver and porcelain, and perhaps Swiss hand-embroidered table mats with serviettes to match.

'Well,' she was murmuring regretfully as she entered her room and closed the door behind her, 'I shan't be having dinner with him in his chalet now, for I'm sure he won't ever ask me again.'

It was barely nine o'clock when Doug telephoned her; she had just finished breakfast and although she would have enjoyed a long ramble through the woods of the Heimwehfluh, she had decided she must stay around in order not to miss Doug's call.

Ernst came to her, his expression faintly enquiring, and informed her that she was wanted on the telephone.

'The caller is a Herr Stouri from Bern,' he added.

'Thank you, Ernst. I'll take it in my room.'

'Very good, Miss Hartnell.' He smiled, but faintly.

Keri was fully aware of his curiosity and saw the wisdom of Doug's strategem.

It was a businesslike voice that greeted her a few moments later when she had lifted the receiver. She was unable to recognize the voice as belonging to Doug, for he had not only acquired an accent but had set his tone at a higher pitch than normal. Ernst knew Doug's voice well, but if he did happen to be listening in he would never place this voice.

Keri was told about the car and informed that she could see it the following afternoon at two o'clock. She thanked him and said she would be there.

'I shall look forward to seeing you, Miss Hartnell,' said the accented voice, 'and hope that we shall be able to do business. I'm sure the car is just what you have been looking for. It's in very good condition.'

She replaced the receiver, not realizing that Paul might also have overheard, from his office. But he had, and when she came down again he frowned and asked her why she was buying a secondhand car.

'I happened to pick up the receiver intending to make a call,' he explained, 'and you were speaking or, at least, I just caught the end of what you were saying, and then some man spoke about a car—a car in very good condition, so it was obviously secondhand.'

Keri, put out of countenance by this unexpected occurrence, was for a moment at a loss for words. But eventually she told him that she had decided to buy a car—just a small one—so that she could get about more easily.

'It'll save taking a taxi all the time,' she added on noting his frown.

'But—a secondhand car?' He looked down at her with an odd expression, 'If you must have a car then

102

why not a new one?'

Keri moistened her lips, again unable to produce an immediate reply. Paul was looking most suspiciously at her, as well he might, she thought, since it was most unlikely that she would even consider a secondhand car, not with her being so able to afford a new one.

'I—er—thought that a secondhand one would do until I get used to the roads around here—I mean, you drive on the right, and I'm not used to that.'

He said nothing for a moment, seeming to be trying to make some sense out of this.

'You can drive, then?' was all he said, and Keri told him that a friend had taught her, and she had passed her test, but of course she had never been able to afford a car of her own. Paul shook his head, a gesture that portrayed both impatience and bewilderment.

'You would be better with a new car,' was his advice, and Keri promised that she would consider this. 'Good,' he approved, and then, after a slight pause, 'I have been thinking, Keri, it will be convenient next week for me to take you on that little tour we mentioned.'

'To see the other hotels?'

He nodded his head.

'Yes. I'll let you know what day, but I rather think it will be Tuesday.'

She smiled happily, flushing a little. Paul's eyes regarded her for some seconds, and they did flicker in the most curious way, she thought. He looked softer, too, and she wondered if it were what he was wearing. He had on a pair of blue slacks and a checked shirt, open at the neck. Casually attired like this he certainly did appear much more human—especially when he smiled in that very attractive way.

'Tuesday,' she repeated shyly. 'That will suit me very well, Paul.'

'We'll set off early and then we might be able to get back by late on Wednesday evening.' He pursed his lips, becoming thoughtful. 'No, I rather think it will be Thursday before we get back.'

'That's all right with me. Shall we stay at our own hotel?'

'I hope so. They're usually fully booked at this time of the year, but I daresay we shall be accommodated.'

When he had left her Keri strolled out to the garden. Guests were sunbathing on the lawn or sitting under the shade of the great cedar tree that stood magnificently on one side of the lawn. Other guests were in the swimming pool, others just walking, admiring the scenery or the beautifully laid-out gardens. Behind and above there rose the stately giant peaks, gleaming in the sunshine. A daunting spectacle, thought Keri, raising her eyes to the breathtaking realm of snow and ice that towered above the valley of the beautiful Lüchine River. Doug had told her something about the geology of the region, of how the unrivalled splendour of the north wall of the Oberland was the result of a vast fault in the rocks which had been caused by a gigantic slip in very ancient times—long before man had appeared on the earth. This slip had caused an overthrust which brought the primordial igneous rocks to the surface.

'And so,' Doug had explained, 'we have this particular type of scenery. But then we have to remember also what the ice has done in carving the land. Ice is so powerful that, in the form of a glacier, it can grind away enormous amounts of rocks, sculpturing the mountains into the shapes which you see here—the horns and the arêtes, the corries and those great crevasses that are so often found in the corrie glaciers.'

'Hello, Miss Hartnell!' The friendly voice of Mr Portman cut into her thoughts and she stopped. He was just coming from the woods that formed part of the great park of the castle. 'You going for a ramble?'

'I'm not sure,' she smiled. 'The woods look inviting.'

'I've had a good stroll; the slopes are sunny higher up, and there are some very pretty flowers.'

She nodded and said yes, she had already seen some of the flowers.

'There are ever so many different ones, aren't there?' she added, feeling that Mr Portman was hoping for her to stand and chat for a little while. 'The cyclamen are prolific in the beech woods over there.'

'And the gentians—they're real pretty. Yes, as you say, there are so many different kinds.'

And most of them protected, thought Keri, just as they should be. She herself could never understand those people who picked wild flowers, for they were taking the seeds; so it was no wonder the flowers had to be protected.

'Well, Miss Hartnell,' Mr Portman was saying a few minutes later, 'I expect you want to be off.'

She was relieved when he had gone; she wanted to be alone, and to think. Some short distance into the woods was a seat almost hidden by bushes and the drooping branches of trees; it was a favourite spot of hers and she found herself wandering in its direction. She had been sitting there for a mere five minutes or so when suddenly she stiffened on hearing the voices of Gena and Ernst. Where they were she could not make out, but that they were somewhere close was certain, for Keri heard all that they were saying.

105

'I had to keep her away from you, Gena.' Ernst spoke in English even though Gena would have understood him had he spoken in German. 'It wouldn't have done had you revealed all to her at that time—or at any time yet.'

'I was in a temper,' she admitted. 'She riles me with her airs and her reminders that she's my employer!'

'I don't think she does it intentionally,' returned Ernst soothingly. 'You yourself don't help the situation.'

Keri's senses tingled; that they were talking about her was clear ... and that the mystery might be explained suggested itself to her—explained, that was, if she continued to listen.

'Did she suspect that you were keeping her from meeting me at that particular time?' Gena's voice was faintly anxious, but Ernst reassured her by saying that he was certain that Keri had not noticed anything which could have aroused her suspicions.

'She had no reason to be suspicious,' he added. 'We've been so careful up till now, and that's why I kept her talking until you'd gone off duty. You'd threatened to disclose the truth to her and I knew it would not have done. I was also sure that once your temper had subsided you yourself would be grateful for my action.'

'Yes, I am grateful. It's too early for her to learn the truth. Yet I sometimes feel that I can't stand the girl a moment longer and I have the greatest difficulty in preventing myself from telling her that she has no right here——'

'Gena,' broke in Ernst warningly, 'you talk far too loudly—and without due care. Supposing Paul were to hear you? You know very well that these woods are a favourite haunt of his.' He continued speaking in this warning vein, but Keri lost his words as, occupying her mind to the exclusion of all else were the words of Gena's,

'... she has no right here. ...' What did it mean? So many incidents came crowding in: Gena's arrogant attitude when speaking to her; the occasion when Gena stated that Paul was the owner of the hotel; on that occasion Gena had sneered at Keri as she made the comment, 'You, Miss Hartnell, are very sure of yourself, aren't you?' And when it seemed that Gena would say more Ernst had intervened to give the warning, 'Be careful, Gena.' Keri had known instantly that the two had shared a secret, but at that time she had no notion that it could be anything of major importance. She had, however, experienced a vague uneasiness and recalled that first impression that Gena Curbishly was to play an important part in her life.

Keri was now certain that her impression was correct. Gena Curbishly *was* to play an important part in her life. But in what way? Here was the puzzle . . . and the mystery. And what about the attitude of Paul himself? There had been several occasions when Keri had been perplexed by his manner.

'... she has no right here. ...' Again Keri's mind was totally occupied by this sentence. It hammered itself into her brain, and she subconsciously repeated it over and over again, her heart pounding against her ribs.

'Paul will not be walking at this time of day!' Gena's voice, raised and impatient, broke gratingly into Keri's confused mind. 'So for goodness' sake, Ernst, stop harping on the possibility!'

'Very well,' mildly and unhurriedly. 'But we did come out here to talk in private——'

'We are private! Who on earth will be here at this time? Some of the guests have hardly finished their breakfasts!'

'True—but you can't be too careful. Many of our guests like walking, and these woods are so handy.' There was no response from Gena and Ernst spoke again. But Keri could not catch his words, for he, unlike Gena, was guarded in his tone, keeping it in a fairly low pitch. Gena, however, could be heard quite plainly and Keri felt her nerve-ends prickle as she caught the words,

'Paul is not altogether stupid, Ernst. He is quite likely to have some small suspicion that I have a secret.'

'You think so?' with some surprise. 'But how can he know about—about ...?' Again his voice was pitched so low that Keri could not hear, no matter how she strained her ears. She bit her lip till it hurt, so vexed was she that this vital piece of information was not to be hers.

'He knows that I was there when it happened.'

'He saw you?'

'No, he didn't actually see me, but when he came from the room I was in the lobby. But I've told you all this, Ernst, when first I asked for your help.'

'Yes, you have told it to me. As for my help, Gena, I sometimes wonder if I am any help at all.' A pause and then, 'You'll give me my rake-off, just the same?' He sounded anxious, Keri thought, the expression 'rake-off' spinning in her mind. What could it mean? Just what were these conspirators up to?

'I never go back on my word,' was the arrogant rejoinder from the girl. 'You shall have what I promised.'

'Thanks. I suppose I have been of some assistance,'

went on Ernst inconsistently after a pause. 'I told you all you wanted to know about the girl's father, and the family background, as it were. I gave you details of her mother.'

'Which you had from that silly old fool with the accent which one can scarcely understand. The fellow Bill from Lancashire!'

'If I can understand him you should be able to do so.'

'I never speak to such people, not if I can help it! You seem to forget just who I am!' The tone was loud and imperious. It came clearly to Keri and she thought that it must be as clear to anyone else who might happen to be wandering hereabouts in the woods. 'I am fully intending to be queen of the castle! I intended to be that immediately on setting foot within its walls!'

'I am not likely to forget who you are,' returned Ernst not without a hint of amused contempt. 'You remind me of it all the time. You are a direct descendant of the builder of the castle. But, Gena, that was all a long, long time ago, and if you hadn't followed that trend that is all the rage in your country you'd never have known about this ancestry of yours. You would have been satisfied with your lot instead of deciding to come over here and look at the castle which had once been in your family.'

'I always knew I was above the average! It did not surprise me at all to discover that I ought to be in a most exalted position! Yes, I did follow the trend and decide to trace my ancestry because I believe that everyone should know who they are. I myself answered an advertisement in the *Sunday Times,* as I mentioned to you. This firm would trace one's ancestry——'
Breaking off, Gena laughed, and Keri flinched. The laugh was grating and arrogant . . . it was also the laugh

of someone who sounded somewhat unbalanced, decided Keri, one half of her mind still held by words which rang repeatedly through it: '... she has no right to be here....' 'Little did I know,' Gena was continuing, 'what the outcome of my expenditure would be. I recall that a colleague of mine in the office said I was mad to waste my money on such things. But how well it's paid off! As soon as I knew who I was I came here, and applied for a job——'

'But what exactly had you in mind, Gena?'

'I'd already discovered that the castle was an hotel—how I hated that idea! However, I also discovered that this would help me to get inside, simply because I could ask for a post of some kind—these hoteliers are always on the look-out for people like me who are highly educated and who can speak several languages. I speak four, as you know. What I had in mind exactly I do not know. I simply wanted to get inside my home, to live in it!' Again a laugh. Keri frowned heavily; the girl was surely not quite right in her mind. Why, many people had found that they were descended from exalted personages, but they did not go to the lengths to which Gena Curbishly had gone.

'But once you were installed and had discovered the attractions of your employer....' Ernst allowed his voice to fade out, but the amused contempt had still been present in it.

'I admit that he did attract me and I mean to marry him, as I've already told you. I mean to be queen!—this is my right!' She paused and for one terrified moment Keri wondered if the couple would move, deciding to carry on with their walk. In which case she would in all probability be discovered. She was well screened, that was true, but a gap in the bushes would reveal her presence to anyone who happened to be passing it. To her relief Gena spoke again, declaring that the castle should—once she was married to Paul— be returned to its former glory as a private residence. 'Paul can keep all his other hotels, for the castle will run away with a great yearly expenditure.'

'You're very sure about becoming Paul's wife, aren't you?'

A low triumphant laugh and then,

'I'd rather he fell in love with me, of course—but, my dear Ernst, if he does not do so it's really of no matter. He shall then marry me because it is my will that he should.'

'You really believe you can force a man like Paul to obey your will?' The sceptical note in Ernst's voice could not be missed and Gena's voice was more imperious and arrogant than ever as he returned,

'I have the whip hand; I hold every ace!'

Every ace. . . . Keri's nerve-ends tingled at this wording. For hadn't she herself gained the odd impression that Gena held all the aces, and that she knew exactly how to use them.

'You'll tell him what you know?'

'If need be! I'm not having that stupid girl hanging around here indefinitely! And supposing she marries? What then? We'd have her husband too. No, she must go—and without too much delay!'

White to the lips now, Keri felt she did not want to hear any more. She felt ill and drained, and very much alone.

But, more than her own misery, there was in her mind the thought of Paul, and this hold which Gena had over him, a hold of which he was at present ignorant, but which Keri knew was of dire importance.

Gena had said she had the whip hand, that she could force Paul to marry her.

'What can she know about him that gives her such power?' murmured Keri in trembling tones as she rose to go back to the gardens of the hotel.

She was still white as she entered the hall; the relief at the desk smiled at her, but she did not see him. And she was staring so blindly ahead that she almost bumped into Mr Portman who was crossing the hall towards the french window.

'Something wrong, Miss Hartnell?' he enquired in some concern. 'Are you ill?'

Dazedly she shook her head.

'No ... no, Mr Portman, I'm fine ... thank you....' She had wandered on, but Paul, having come round the corner from the lobby, had stood and listened to her conversation with Mr Portman.

'Keri,' he called as she made her progression towards the stairs. 'Keri!'

She turned, her foot on the first stair.

'Yes, Paul?'

He eyed her searchingly, a frown knitting his brow.

'Are you sure you're not ill?'

'I rather think that she is,' interposed Mr Portman, taking a few steps to bring him closer to Paul. 'I've never seen anyone quite so pale as she is.'

'I'm fine—really I am.'

'But you don't look fine,' objected Mr Portman before Paul could speak. 'You look as if you've had a terrible shock.'

Her eyes, glazed and staring, passed both him and Paul.

'I have a headache, that is all,' she said impatiently. 'I'm going to my room——'

'A headache?' interrupted Paul, still frowning and still subjecting her to that searching regard, 'but you just assured us that you were fine.'

She swallowed hard, wondering how she could escape from his all-seeing gaze.

'I want to go to my room!' she cried at last in a strangled tone. 'And what's more, I'm going! So please, Paul, go away and leave me alone!'

He stared, as well he might. Mr Portman murmured something about getting a doctor. Keri turned and ran up the stairs, her one desire being to talk to Doug before she talked to Paul. She needed advice, and help, and it was Doug and not Paul to whom she wanted to turn. He was practical and he would listen with understanding, especially if he himself had, last night, learned something from listening in to the conversation of Gena and Ernst.

She would have liked to see him this evening, after he had returned from taking his party out on a tour, but as he had told her to meet him at two the following day she felt disinclined to upset his plans.

'It'll seem like years,' she said quiveringly as she lay down on the bed, aware that she had told the truth when she said she had a headache. In fact, her head was throbbing and she got up to find the aspirins. A couple of the tablets would not only cure her headache but send her to sleep, she thought. And she was right. Her mind became hazy and soon she had fallen into a restful slumber.

It did her so much good that when, later, she appeared at the lunch table she was much more like her normal self. Paul, having asked that when she reappeared he was to be informed, came from his office and sat down at her table, obviously intending to take

113

lunch with her.

'You look much better,' he observed, but she felt certain that she detected a note of anxiety in his voice as he added, 'There was something the matter earlier, wasn't there, Keri?'

She looked at him across the table.

'I had a headache,' she murmured, avoiding his eyes as they began to narrow. 'It was the truth, Paul, really.'

'Perhaps, but there was something else. Do you feel like telling me what it was?' He sounded kind, and persuasive, and she liked his mood; it was the sort of mood to which in normal circumstances she would so readily have responded—but not now. It was still Doug she wanted.

'It was nothing,' she told him, and her heart sank as his expression changed.

'Then I must accept that,' he returned coldly and, rising from his chair, he told her that he was lunching at home. 'I'll be here for dinner,' he added curtly and, turning on his heel, he strode from the restaurant.

CHAPTER SEVEN

Doug was already at the landing-stage when Keri arrived, although she herself was ten minutes early. Eagerly she scanned his face and obligingly he nodded, grinning in that familiar manner and saying he would tell her everything once they were on board and had found a quiet spot up on the top deck. He had already

114

bought the tickets, so they boarded the ship at once, the lovely Iseltwald, shining white in the clear sunshine. The lake itself was glistening, the mountains reflected in its waters. Many holidaymakers came aboard, but Doug and Keri managed to remain secluded and Doug began at once to relate what had happened after he had left her.

'I managed to smuggle myself into that corner and began rearranging the scenery, keeping one eye on the waiter—who, by the way, never so much as batted an eyelid on seeing me sitting there, all ready for another meal.'

'Did you have one?' she asked, diverted even though she was impatient to hear what he had to say, and even more impatient to relate her own story.

'No, as a matter of fact I merely had a snack.' He then went on immediately to tell her that he had not been able to overhear all that the couple were saying, but he had heard quite enough to convince him that they were a pair of conspirators, and a nasty pair at that. 'They know something about Paul von Hasler, something which can get him into some trouble.'

'What kind of trouble, Doug?' She knew a terrible fear—and wondered deeply at the reason for it. Why should she have such strong emotions as this over a man who was only her business partner?

'I couldn't get it at all. What I did get was that Gena aspires to become Paul's wife, that she has sufficient knowledge to force him into marriage if he shouldn't willingly offer to marry her.'

'This is dreadful!' Keri's face was pale and Doug frowned heavily.

'Does it matter all that much to you?' was his curious enquiry.

115

'It matters that he might be in serious trouble, yes, of course it does. After all, he's my business partner.'

'I see. . . .' A pause and then, 'You yourself have some news. I saw it at once in your expression,' he added when she gave an involuntary start of surprise. 'I'm quick at reading expressions,' he ended with a return of that cheerful grin. 'Talk away, Keri, it'll make you feel better.'

'I doubt it,' she responded, but continued to speak before he could interrupt to ask why she doubted it.

Her story took less than ten minutes to relate, but during that time Doug's expression changed over and over again. On occasions he would open his eyes wide, on others a heavy frown would settle on his brow. Sometimes he would seem to gasp inwardly, and at others he would bite his lip, as if he did not like to hear what she was saying.

'Well, what do you make of it all?' she asked when, after hearing her out, Doug sat there, his brow furrowed in thought, not offering any immediate comment. 'Why should she say that I have no right at the castle?'

Another silence and then, looking at her with what could only be described as an anxious expression, he asked,

'When you came to the castle, how did Paul receive you?'

The question seemed to be faintly evasive, as if Doug was turning something over in his mind and he was not willing to divulge this at the present time. He appeared to be requiring a period of conjecture before coming to a conclusion.

'He knew beforehand that I should be coming——'

'Yes, I realize that,' interrupted Doug with a hint of impatience. 'Naturally he would be expecting you.

116

But what kind of a reception did he give you?'

'He was cool, but not in any way unfriendly. Doug,' she said a trifle breathlessly, 'why do you ask that? Has it anything to do with what Gena said—about my having no right at the castle, that is?'

'I can't say very much at this stage, Keri,' he told her after a moment's consideration. 'I must put all this information into some sort of order. Please do not expect too much at this stage.'

'But——'

'We'll talk, yes, I know you have much to ask and it's only natural that you would be glad of answers, but as I've said, I cannot arrive at points in a hurry. When I've had time I shall probably be able to answer at least some of your questions.' He looked at her with a mingling of apology and firmness. She had quietly,

'I suppose I must be patient—I really have no alternative,' she added as the thought occurred to her. Doug nodded and reverted to the question he had previously asked.

'You say that Paul was cool but not unfriendly. But can you say for sure that he welcomed you?' Doug was looking intently at her as this question was put.

'No,' she replied frankly, 'he did not welcome me. You see, he had previously offered to buy me out and I had agreed—through my solicitor in England, that was. But I later changed my mind and decided to take up my father's position, having in mind that I could learn enough about the business to enable me to help in the running of it. Paul was not too pleased at this change of mind, which was understandable, I suppose, since he had been assured of my compliance with his offer. He had become used to the idea that he was soon to be sole owner of the business.' As she was talking

Doug was nodding his head.

'I think,' he said slowly, and so softly that she gained the idea that he was merely speaking his thoughts aloud, 'that you would have been wiser to have sold out to him.'

She frowned.

'What makes you say that, Doug?' She was so bewildered that she could not think properly and her anger was rising at the idea that Doug should have said a thing like this. 'I'm quite capable of learning——'

'Don't get my meaning wrong,' he broke in to advise her. 'I'm not underrating your intelligence; I'm merely stating what I believe is a fact: you would have been wiser to have kept to your original decision and sold out to him.' A pause and then, noting her state of bewilderment and perplexity, 'Paul must have had a very good reason for wanting to buy you out.'

'He wanted full control of the business.'

'That could be one reason,' he agreed.

'But in your opinion he had an altogether different reason?'

'I believe so, yes.' Another pause. 'What are your conclusions regarding his character?'

'His character? What has that to do with it——?'

'Keri, my girl, just sit there and pretend that I'm a detective and you are being questioned by me. We'll get much farther in a much quicker time if you will do this.'

She nodded, admitting herself that they were not making much progress as things were.

'Very well, Doug, I'll do as you say.'

'Good girl.' He became thoughtful again, and his eyes wandered to the lakeside. The ship was just entering the lake proper, having sailed a short distance along the River Aare. 'Tell me how his character strikes you?' he asked again, and she was spontaneous in her reply this time, saying that Paul was an honourable man, totally upright and a man to be trusted, a stickler for fair play. And in order to illustrate this latter statement Keri told Doug about Bill, and the way Paul had not only raised his wages but had also paid him all the money which in his opinion Bill should have been given in those earlier years.

'I'd like to have a long talk with Bill,' Doug murmured when she had finished speaking. 'However, for the present I am keenly interested in your assessment of Paul's character—and particularly interested in this mention of fair play. It would appear that, should someone not play fair, then Paul would endeavour to put right any injustices that might have occurred as a result of this.'

Keri nodded, one part of her mind absorbed by the fact of Paul's having put right the injustice done to Bill, but the other part grappling to discover a reason why Doug should be attaching so much importance to this particular aspect of Paul's character.

'I don't understand you, Doug,' she said apologetically, but added straight away, 'However, fire the questions at me if you think the picture will become clearer for you. I'm anxious to know exactly what's going on.' Her thoughts went to Gena, and to the girl's confident assertion that she would marry Paul. She must have been saying much the same thing when she and Ernst had dined at the Metropole, since Doug had also known of this confidence, a confidence resulting from the hold she had over Paul.

'I'm sure you are, Keri.' He spoke soothingly and—

could it be a trifle pityingly? she wondered. Doug went over various points contained in the information she herself had given him. He talked about the way Ernst must have been won over by Gena's promise of a monetary reward for any secrets he could impart to her regarding Paul, and Keri's father. Yes, he continued when Keri looked enquiringly at him, he had overheard Gena and Ernst discussing Mr Hartnell and his eccentric ways. 'Gena came to work at the castle just after your father died, so she wouldn't have any first-hand knowledge of what kind of a man he was. Ernst seems to have given her a complete picture; she knew that your father and Paul had quarrelled regularly.'

Keri was frowning as she listened to all this.

'Why should Gena want to know about my father? It doesn't make sense.'

'Not at present.' Doug was evasive; she was alert to the fact that he knew more than he was at present willing to divulge.

'This thing about Paul. What can she know about him that could give her such power?' She looked at him with a deeply troubled expression. 'That is the question I asked myself on hearing Gena say it.'

'I didn't get it, Keri,' was Doug's quiet reply. 'It's my intention to saunter into the Schloss Raimegen, as I often do for a drink, and then chat to one or two of the people I know best—and to Bill, whom I don't know too well but who always seems to be amicable. In this way I hope to learn something of importance.'

Keri's eyes became pensive and she remained quiet for a while, her senses half absorbed by the beauty around her—the calm lake with its narrow coastal belt of green where colourful chalets nestled, their walls beautifully carved, their gardens ablaze with colour, the waterfalls tumbling down from the mountains, the long drop turning the shining water into a series of lace veils that seemed to quiver in the breeze. And towering above it all the daunting but majestic range of peaks, snow-capped, their serrated edges glittering against a sky of sapphire blue. Lower down were the sunny slopes where cows and sheep grazed the lush green grass. From some buildings along the water's edge flags could be seen waving slightly in the breeze. The Swiss loved flags and would fly them at the least excuse, Doug had told her.

'What I can't understand,' frowned Keri at last, 'is Gena's mentality. When she was speaking about becoming the queen of the castle it sounded ridiculous to me. I gained the impression that she—well—wasn't quite right in her head.'

'She's right in her head, but obsessed by a desire to become a great lady—this owing, of course, to what she discovered about her ancestry. I agree with what you are thinking: that no one with any sense at all would go to the extent of throwing up her job and coming here the way she did. She's obviously irrational to a certain degree,' he added with a sudden frown, and amending what he had said, 'simply because she has allowed herself to become totally absorbed by the desire to live in the castle; she'll go to any lengths to achieve her ends.'

'Any lengths. . . .' Keri thought of Paul and wondered if he would agree to marry Gena. Keri, like Ernst, could not imagine him being intimidated by anyone, but it did seem that Gena could blackmail him into marriage. A shudder passing through her at this idea, she wished she could warn Paul, but her relationship with him being what it was, there never could

121

be an occasion where such an opportunity would arise. 'Paul would never be happy with a girl like Gena,' she added, then coloured. For Doug's eyes had flickered with a look of keen perception.

'You rather like Paul, don't you?' he enquired gently, and she had to say yes, she did like him. 'In spite of his hardness and his refusal to allow you to build a chalet?'

'I'm annoyed about that,' she had to admit. 'But I still like Paul; as I've said, he's an upright and honest man. I also admire his efficiency and his firmness.'

'His firmness?' with a slight lift of the eyebrows. 'So you're one of those delightful females who admire mastery in a man, eh?'

Her colour rising even higher, she said,

'Shall we keep to the investigation, Doug? I must find out what is happening.'

'Well, I shall have to warn you of two things, Keri,' he returned decisively. 'One is that the investigations are going to take some time; the other is——' Here he broke off, hesitating and looking at her with that rather pitying expression which she had noticed before, 'the other is, Keri, that you might be bitterly disappointed with the results of those investigations.'

She looked sharply at him, her heart twisting and then beginning to beat overrate.

'You're warning me of something,' she said, and in her voice was a deep note of depression and urgency. 'What is it? I must know—I must!'

'Steady on,' came his low and soothing response. 'I don't have anything concrete on which to go at the present time——'

'You have suspicions,' she broke in with the same urgency, 'strong suspicions. Also, I believe that you overheard much more than you've told me!'

'At the Metropole, you mean?'

'Of course! Where else would you overhear anything?' She was pale and afraid, and she repeated, more to herself than to him. 'Do I have a right to be at the castle or not? And if not, then how does this come about?'

Doug remained frustratingly silent for what seemed an eternity before saying, in the deliberate unhurried manner he was adopting during this discussion,

'Paul has accepted you as his partner; surely that's proof and enough that you have every right to be at the castle?'

'It should be,' she quivered, 'but somehow I feel that perhaps there's been some mistake—a mistake of which Gena and Ernst are aware.' She was watching Doug closely and she felt almost certain that he had given a slight start at her words. 'I always believed that Father would disinherit me—leave everything to charity.'

'To charity?' he repeated, much too quickly, she thought, but failed to discover a reason for this idea. 'What made you conclude that he would leave it to charity?'

She stared at him; his words had been almost identical to those used by Paul on that first evening when at dinner she had talked of the absence of a will and had told Paul that she had fully expected her father to leave all his wealth to charity.

'There's no one else to whom he could leave it,' she replied, recalling that this was also the answer she had given to Paul. 'I'm his only relative.'

Doug gave a small sigh and looked away, appearing to become absorbed in a number of small yachts which seemed to be getting ready for a race. The people manning them were calling to one another and their voices echoed across the water.

'People do sometimes leave money to people who are not related to them,' came the softly spoken comment after a while.

'I suppose so, but my father didn't have any friends at all, so he couldn't have done that. In any case, the will would have been there, with his lawyer, but it wasn't.'

'I'm not suggesting that he did leave his money to anyone else,' Doug assured her. 'As you say, had he done so, the will would have been with his lawyer.'

Keri, her mind filled with doubts which she could not even begin to understand, would have pursued this line of conversation, asking the reason for the remarks which Doug had just made, but he did not afford her the opportunity as, once again, he plied her with questions. In this way he eventually had before him a full picture of all that had transpired since the moment she had entered the Schloss Raimegen as partner to Paul. He mused over all this for a few moments and then reverted to the conversation which Keri had overheard between Ernst and Gena.

'I'm interested in that part where they were talking about the secret. Gena said, in answer to a question from Ernst, that Paul knew she was there when it happened. I do have that correct, don't I?' He was brisk and businesslike, giving her confidence in his ability to unravel the mystery.

'Yes, you do have it correctly,' she replied, recalling how vexed she had been at not having caught all of what Ernst had said.

'When it happened,' repeated Doug. 'When *what*

happened?—this is what we would like to know more than anything. In fact, it's my belief that the mystery would be entirely cleared up were we to have the answer to this question.'

'Gena said that Paul didn't actually see her there but that he had realized she was in the lobby.'

'Didn't see her in the room, that was,' mused Doug. 'Now—he was in a room doing something which Gena saw. Right?'

'That's the impression I got, and as you've got the same impression I'm sure it's right.'

'So far so good. Paul saw Gena only when he came out to the lobby—that's where she was, but——' Doug wagged a finger thoughtfully, and at no one in particular. 'But,' he continued slowly and almost painstakingly as if each word were being dragged from some far recess of his mind, 'she must have been standing in the open doorway of the room when Paul was doing whatever it was that she saw him doing. She moved swiftly, but not so swiftly that she could escape altogether, hence her being in the passageway on his coming from the room....' His words faded and he frowned darkly to himself. 'Whatever it was that Gena saw was obviously not what an honest upright man would do?' and at this pronouncement he looked directly into Keri's eyes. 'You do realize this much, of course?'

She shook her head; it was a desperate gesture, denoting a refusal to accept what was being put so plainly and so irrefutably before her.

'Paul wouldn't do anything dishonourable—I know it!'

'All right, we'll let that pass for the time being. But you will have to accept that, whatever it was, it provided Gena with knowledge that, used against Paul, would get him into serious trouble.'

Keri shook her head again, but this time it was a gesture of despair. She felt almost ill and asked herself again why she should be so strongly affected by the idea of Paul's being in danger.

'I suppose I must accept it,' she replied unsteadily on noting that Doug was awaiting her reply. 'Yes, I must accept it.' She paused a moment and then, 'Doug, can I ask you something?'

'You're at liberty to ask, my dear, but I can't promise you an answer.'

'I do understand that. However, I'll ask just the same. Have you any idea at all what it was that Paul was doing in that room?'

'Yes, I have an idea—but it's only an idea. In fact, it's merely the germ of an idea, and for that reason I shan't tell you what it is.'

She looked at him, her mouth quivering.

'It—was something—illegal?' she faltered, almost willing Doug to give her a negative reply. But he gave her the reply which was honest, even though he was fully aware of her distress.

'Highly illegal, Keri.'

'He—he c-could be p-put in prison?'

Doug did hesitate then, but on noticing how intently she was regarding him he answered, still in that quiet but businesslike tone,

'I believe so, yes.'

She swallowed the fear that had lodged in the form of a lump in her throat.

'I couldn't bear it,' she cried. 'Oh, Doug, I can only hope and pray that you're very wrong in your deductions!'

He gave a deep sigh.

'I hope so too, my dear Keri, but. . . .'

'But what?' Urgently, demandingly as she looked into his serious blue eyes. 'You know very well that you aren't wrong, don't you?'

He shifted uneasily in his seat before answering her question.

'The fact that Gena has this hold is proof that Paul has done something which he shouldn't have done——'

'But it wasn't a dishonourable act!' she broke in desperately. 'I know for certain that he would *not* act in a manner that was dishonourable!'

'My dear,' said Doug kindly but a trifle impatiently for all that, 'haven't we said that we'll allow this to pass for the time being——? No, please don't interrupt. We *shall* allow it to pass.'

'So I'm to be in misery again tonight?'

'Misery?' he questioned, but Keri made no answer and he added curiously, 'You appear to be suffering much more than is necessary over the fate of your partner.'

She looked away, her mouth trembling, her whole mind on the picture of Paul—handsome, proud, carrying himself like an aristocrat. She saw his straight and frank grey eyes, his firm mouth that could relax and soften with a smile. She felt her heart catch, became aware of the blood flowing far too quickly through her veins. Something strange passed through her consciousness and she tried to capture it, but it eluded her. Nevertheless, she was left with the conviction that it would return and, as she sat there, staring out over the lovely lake towards the thickly-wooded foothills, it did return, and she felt the colour leave her face as the truth was borne in upon her.

Bringing her gaze back to the man opposite to her, she met his penetrating stare. She spoke at last, in tones scarcely above a whisper,

'I care a great deal about what happens to Paul. It will hurt me excruciatingly if he's in trouble.'

'I thought so. Your face is very revealing, Keri.'

She felt the swift return of her colour but made no attempt to turn away from him, nor did she make any denial of what was so obviously plain to him—in fact it now struck her that he had probably made a guess at her feelings for Paul even before she had discovered them herself.

'Have you any more questions to ask me?' she enquired at length, aware that the ship was almost at Brienz.

'I can't think of many,' he replied. 'However, there is one. The room in which Gena saw Paul—you didn't happen to get a clue as to which room it was?'

She frowned and shook her head.

'Does it make any difference?' she asked.

'It could do.'

She was about to ask why, but his expression told her that it would be futile, as she would not receive an answer.

'It would be one of the rooms which are private, wouldn't it?'

'I should imagine so.' Doug looked at her. 'His office ... is it off a lobby?'

'Yes, it is. He has a sitting-room next to it.'

Doug nodded thoughtfully.

'I expect it's a nice cosy place—big fireplace and all that?' He glanced away, interested in the two swans which were swimming close to the edge of the lake.

'Yes, it is cosy, but he doesn't spend much time in

it. I imagine he used it a lot before he had his chalet built in the grounds.'

'Yes, I should imagine he did.' A small pause and then, 'Would it be possible, do you think, for me to see that room?'

She started, shaking her head vigorously.

'If you mean can I let you go in—no, I wouldn't dare. Paul would be furious——'

'My idea was that Paul shouldn't know,' he put in dryly. 'Naturally I'm not going to go poking about when he's there.'

She bit her lip.

'Sorry, that was silly of me—but it was only my phrasing, really. What I meant was that if Paul did happen to come along when I was showing you in. . . .' She shrugged her shoulders, meaning this to be final, but Doug was not to be so easily put off.

'This evening—will he be at the hotel, or over at his chalet?'

'He might be dining with the guests, but he'll go home as soon as dinner is over. He doesn't often stay at the hotel in the evenings.'

'I shall come over. We'll have a drink in the lounge and then wander in the grounds. I want to see that room if it's only from the outside.'

'From the outside? What good will that do?'

'I shall probably be able to see what I want to see,' he told her, adding that this was of course if the curtains were open.

'He closes them before he leaves,' she said, troubled by Doug's insistence and perplexed as to why an inspection of the room should be so important.

'Well, we shall see what we can do.' He stopped and indicated the landing-stage. 'We're there. We'll have a nice cup of coffee and some cakes and then return by bus.'

'You haven't given me any idea as to the reason why Gena should have said that about my having no right to be at the Schloss Raimegen,' she said as they rose to leave the ship. 'You must have some ideas about it, surely?'

'I have, Keri, but I'm in no position to voice those ideas. Be patient, there's a good girl. I shan't keep you waiting any longer than is necessary.'

CHAPTER EIGHT

TRUE to his word, Doug came over to the hotel that evening. He sat in the lounge having a drink and, as arranged before they parted company earlier in the day, Keri sauntered in and, nodding casually, sat down at another table. Gena, glamorous in black and gold, was serving the drinks, and as she knew Doug well she stopped to chat with him for a moment or two. Not so with Keri, whom she kept waiting, not even coming to take her order.

Doug finished his drink and rose as if preparing to go, but instead he came casually towards Keri and on reaching her table said smilingly,

'Good evening, Miss Hartnell. Shall I see you on the Lucerne trip tomorrow?'

She nodded her head, responding to his smile,

'Yes, I shall be with Luise.' Her eyes wandered to

Gena, who was deliberately loitering by the next table, intent on listening to what was being said.

'May I sit down for a moment?' asked Doug. 'I've suddenly decided that I'd like another drink.'

'Of course you can sit down.'

'Thanks.'

It was all so cool and polite, leaving Gena with the impression that the two were mere acquaintances who had met once or twice when on the tours.

Gena came, because she had to, and took the order from Doug. On her return with the drinks he adopted a teasing manner and said,

'Aren't I honoured, sitting here with the young lady who owns half this magnificent castle?'

Keri held her breath; Doug had not warned her of this. Gena's face seemed to twist into evil lines and she did appear as a woman who was slightly demented, Keri thought. The dark eyes blazed, the mouth compressed and yet moved slightly as if its owner was caught in the net of some deep emotion.

'I suppose you are.' Low the tone but venomous as the hiss of a snake. And without affording Doug any opportunity of speaking again she swept away from the table, spilling the liquid in one of the glasses as she did so.

'Doug,' whispered Keri while the woman's back was to them, 'surely that was dangerous?'

'I wanted to see her reaction. That *woman* is dangerous!' His eyes were narrowed as they followed the girl until she disappeared through the archway. 'Yes, very dangerous.' Keri said nothing, her mind too confused for her to make any contribution towards a conversation. If she spoke at all it would be to ask questions,

131

and she knew full well that Doug would not answer them.

When the drinks were finished he rose and as Gena was not about both he and Keri left the lounge together. Once outside, in the darkness of the grounds, he asked to be taken to Paul's private sitting-room.

'It's round the other side,' she began. 'But, Doug, supposing he's in the grounds, strolling about?'

'We'll be careful. Don't worry, I shall see him before he sees us. And there are plenty of bushes where we can hide.'

She said nothing more in protest but took him at once to the window of Paul's room. And as it happened the curtains had not been closed.

'Ah!' he exclaimed with satisfaction. 'Just what I wanted.' With a quick glance around to make sure that no one was anywhere near, Doug went to the window and peered through it. Watching his dark silhouette Keri saw him nod his head. She heard him give a small sigh before, turning to her, he said cryptically, 'I thought so. I'm very satisfied with what I've seen.' And yet his voice held a note that was distinctly regretful, and Keri felt certain that, could she have seen his expression, it would have reflected this same regret.

'What have you seen, Doug?' she asked beseechingly. Please enlighten me—just a little.'

'Impossible, Keri, because it's still all conjecture——'

'But the pieces of the puzzle are falling into place?'

'They appear to be, and yet they could be the wrong pieces. I shan't know until the whole of the pieces are in place.'

She remained silent, but her dejection was obvious and Doug tucked his arm into hers in a comforting gesture.

'I'm sorry to be like this.' She turned her head and it came close to his shoulder. 'It's so worrying, and in spite of what you say, Doug, it would make me feel much better if you told me what it is that you've discovered up till now.'

'I believe,' he returned gently, 'it would not only be wrong of me to confide in you at this time, but criminal. You see, Keri dear, it's all conjecture, and it's such that it would cause you grave and unnecessary anxiety——'

'Anxiety for myself or for Paul?' she wanted to know, and he answered quietly,

'Both, Keri.'

'I see....'

'Consequent on this anxiety would come the inability to keep silent, and total secrecy is imperative if I'm to solve the mystery. No one—I repeat, *no one*, must suspect for one moment that you know anything at all. Understand?'

She nodded meekly, thinking how very different he was in this mood from that which he had adopted on their first meeting. Then he was gay and appeared to be a man who lived for the most part on the surface of life, skating along merrily without any thought for the tumbles. But she now knew that he had a much more serious side to his character, and she was grateful that he had shown it to her, in his offer of help in unravelling the mystery which she on her own would have continued to find baffling.

'Yes, Doug,' she replied when, having stopped, he was waiting for her answer. They were close to some magnolia trees, and these trees were in turn at the end of a narrow rustic bridge that spanned a tiny stream, a tributary of the Lüchine River. Starlight was reflected in the stream, and a little distance away a fountain also glittered faintly. It was an idyllic place, she thought, here in the castle grounds with its gigantic trees darkly etched against the night sky, and the pointed turrets also sharply outlined, tall and noble and yet puny in comparison to the immense tangled peaks and glaciers of the Oberland which rose in awesome majesty to the purple starlit sky. 'How wonderful it all is,' she breathed, and her thoughts were with Paul, and she wished it were he who was here with her, in this magic place which seemed to have been created for lovers. She sighed unknowingly and Doug said,

'What was that for—such a deep sigh?'

'I'm unhappy, Doug,' she answered, and before she could control the impulse she was weeping on his shoulder.

'Dear Keri. . . .' His tones held a wealth of sympathy and compassion. 'Child, why didn't you sell out to him instead of coming here?'

'I sh-should have d-done,' she quivered. 'I know it now, but it's too late.'

'It's not too late——' He stopped, and thought for a moment. 'Would you consider selling out?' he asked, and she felt certain that she detected a note of urgency in his tone.

'I really don't know.'

'It would be wise—No, don't ask me why. I'm giving you advice, Keri. Think about it and we'll talk again tomorrow.' She made no answer and he added, 'Promise me that you'll think about it.'

'All right, I will.' But she was still in tears and Doug held her comfortingly.

'Don't cry,' he murmured softly. 'It could all come

134

right in the end.'

She dwelt on these words of Doug's long after he had left her. She had gone straight up to her bedroom but, fully convinced that she would not sleep, she made no attempt to go to bed. Instead she sat in the armchair and dejectedly went over all that had been said that day. It was plain that Doug was well on the way to solving the mystery; it was equally plain that he was troubled as to how the outcome was to affect Keri herself. She could not but guess that something was drastically wrong regarding her position as partner to Paul, and over and over again there was repeated in her mind that conviction that her father would leave his money away from her.

She sighed and made an effort to dismiss all these frustrating circumstances from her thoughts, but they persisted in crowding in and Gena would appear, then Ernst, and then Paul himself, aloof, dignified; and it seemed quite impossible that he could be involved in anything that was not strictly legal.

Her thoughts were eventually cut by the telephone ringing and, puzzled, she lifted the receiver. It was Paul.

'I knew you were still up,' he told her, 'because I saw that your light was on. I've rung to tell you that we shall be starting on our little trip first thing in the morning.' He sounded friendly, almost eager to take her on this trip to see the other properties. His voice was cool and confident as always and somehow she was almost totally reassured.

'Tomorrow?' She thought of Doug and that he would be expecting her to be with Luise on the coach.

'Yes. It's convenient?'

'I was intending to accompany Luise, but——'

135

'Luise doesn't need you, Keri. Be ready at eight if you can.'

'Very well, Paul, I'll be ready—and thank you for offering to take me.'

'It'll be a pleasure—and a break for me. I did say I wouldn't be able to manage it so soon, but by a little rearranging I find I can fit it in very well.' He ended by asking if she had bought the car, and when she said no he bade her good night and replaced the receiver. Keri stood for a moment, a smile coming to her lips. He had said it would be a pleasure.... And she knew by his tone that he meant it. Suddenly she was happy, for if all was not right then why should Paul be so willing to take her on this trip?

'I do belong here!' she said firmly. 'It's Gena who shall go!'

The sun was shining brilliantly when, promptly at eight o'clock the following morning, Paul had the car at the front of the hotel. Keri, looking casual in a bright cotton dress and sandals, with her hair newly washed and shining, had made sure she did not keep him waiting. She had ordered her breakfast to be brought up to her room so that she could be drying her hair while she ate her eggs and toast. And she was in the hall by five minutes to eight.

'You're off somewhere this morning, Miss Hartnell?' It was Ernst who spoke. Having been on duty all night, he was waiting for the appearance of Gena. 'You're bright and early.' Curiously his eyes slid to the suitcase by her side.

She nodded and replied in cool impersonal accents,

'Yes, Ernst, I am off somewhere this morning.' That was all, and if he were taken aback then she was glad, she told herself. She was standing some few paces from the desk, one eye on the glass door through which she would see the car appear from the direction of the garage where Paul kept it.

Gena appeared, looked with surprise at Keri, then turned an enquiring eye towards Ernst. But he said nothing more than a few brief words of greeting and Keri noticed, not without some considerable satisfaction, that Gena was extremely puzzled by this early start which Keri was obviously intending to make, and looking so happy about it!

'I understood you were accompanying Luise,' she said, and Keri had to smile to herself, for it was so very plain that the girl could not contain her curiosity.

'My plans are changed,' replied Keri in short and icy tones. 'Will you have a porter come to me?'

'A porter——' Gena stopped as she caught sight of the suitcase, which Keri had moved, placing it beside a potted palm, and so it had not been obvious to Gena as it had to Ernst. 'Yes ... of course.'

'Thank you.' Keri glanced towards the door and now she saw the car drawing up close to the steps. She ran lightly down and Paul, having slid from the car, held open the door for her to get in.

'You've packed some clothes?' He looked faintly anxious as he glanced up towards the entrance. 'You knew we'd be away for a couple of days or so.' He stopped, for at this moment Bill appeared carrying the case. He smiled at Keri and said,

'Morning, Miss Hartnell. Have a good trip.'

'Thank you, Bill,' she returned, aware of his puzzlement. He had no idea where she was going and yet he had wished her a good trip. She wondered what kind of a conversation would be carried on in the porters' room when he got back with this information.

The suitcase was in the boot and Paul back in the driver's seat.

'Well, we're off,' he said, letting in the clutch. 'You haven't forgotten anything?'

Keri shook her head.

'No, nothing.' She felt shy and a little unsure of herself—very different from the way she had been with him on previous occasions when their wills had clashed. 'Where are we going first?'

'Lucerne. As you know, we have two hotels there. Then we shall go to Neuchâtel and then to Basle where we shall stay the night.'

'Do we have an hotel at Basle?'

'We have two.' Paul was driving out through the massive gateway and Keri glanced back. The lovely white castle shone in the summer sunlight, its red roof and red-topped turrets sharply outlined against the sapphire sky. Tall majestic cedars massed behind it and to one side gave it that fairy-tale appearance which had impressed her so deeply all those years ago, and she sighed a little regretfully at the thought that all had not come out as she had hoped; for she had looked forward with such eagerness to a full and satisfying life with her new partner. She now wondered how she would feel if she had to leave it—But no, she would never have to leave it! She would not think of Gena's neurotic utterings, for they could not possibly have any foundations.

'Just look down the valley,' Paul was saying, and as always she gasped at the view—the lovely flat-floored valley with its lush green pastures reaching well up the sides, the groves of copper beech contrasting with the darker clumps of pine trees which grew on the higher reaches of the valley sides. A silvery stream meandered through the floor, its banks ablaze with golden flowers. From the mountain-sides with their amazing array of different shades of green, there tumbled many streams, hanging valleys left by the ice when it retreated and now forming waterfalls which, fed by the glaciers as they slowly melted, plunged down to join the river thousands of feet below. Some of these cascades looked as if they were actually touching the chalets built all along the valley sides, picturesque wooden chalets ornamented with bright little figures in niches and flower-filled window boxes.

'It's very beautiful,' she breathed at last. 'I say this to myself each time I look at this particular view.'

'Strangely, so do I?' he replied, turning swiftly to give her a smile. 'I've lived here for a number of years, but the view still gives me a great deal of pleasure.' He was driving carefully but in a manner of leisurely unconcern. It did not seem possible that a shadow loomed over him, and suddenly Keri, reassured because of this attitude of his, felt inordinately happy and free from care. Something deep inside her seemed to be telling her to put aside all apprehensions and alarms and to enjoy to the full these few days with Paul. He was in a friendly mood, an approachable mood, and she desired only to bask for a while in this most pleasant atmosphere, remembering how she had, right from the first, wished to be Paul's friend. Friend.... A small sigh escaped her as she visualized the future, alone, for she now knew she would never marry, not loving Paul the way she did.

'You haven't yet been to Lucerne?' Paul was asking, and Keri shook her head.

'No; I could have gone on the tour last Monday, but

I decided against it.'

'You did? Why?'

'I wasn't needed, and I do sometimes wonder if Luise and Emma get a little tired of having me around.'

'They don't act in an unfriendly way, surely?'

'Oh, no, not at all! On the contrary, they're charming, and helpful, but I sometimes feel that I'm only in the way.'

'You still want to do some more useful work, I suppose?'

'I'd like to, yes, but if it isn't possible I suppose I must be satisfied with the job I have.'

'You sound resigned.' He looked curiously at her, slowing down as he reached the main street of Wilderswil.

'I'm not pushing anything at the present time,' she told him quietly, and then she changed the subject, for she was very much afraid that Paul would question her further. She asked about the hotels at Lucerne and Paul obligingly gave her an outline of their location and explained the lines on which they were run.

'You have very efficient managers,' she commented when at length he stopped speaking. 'Did you choose them or did Father?'

He smiled and she knew the answer even before he said,

'I chose them, Keri.'

'Father wouldn't have found such good ones?'

'He was English, you see, and he did not trouble to learn our language even though he lived here for so long. And it's not easy to negotiate, as it were, if you speak a different tongue.'

Keri opened her mouth to say that these men who applied for posts of hotel managers must be required

140

to speak several languages, but then she realized that Paul had merely used this explanation as an excuse, and that the real explanation was that her father would have used arrogance and bombast where politeness and finesse were required.

'Tell me some more,' she urged. 'What sort of people stay at our hotels in Lucerne?'

'All sorts,' he said with some amusement. 'How can one differentiate?'

'It was a silly question, then?'

'You are showing interest, Keri, and that is the important thing.' He spoke kindly, bypassing her query in the nicest possible way. 'We get many people from Britain, especially during the months of July and August. They often leave their marks behind—unfortunately.'

'Marks?'

'Your people appear to have a craze for carving their names all over the place. In one of our hotels at Lucerne we had to renew all the backs of the rustic seats we'd put in the garden, for a party of forty odd people had defaced them by carving their names on them with penknives or some such implements.'

'All of them!' gasped Keri, feeling ashamed that her people could cause such destruction. 'They *all* carved their names?'

'I don't expect the women did—not the older ones, that is. But the men—well, they weren't satisfied with doing it once; we had the same names carved on half a dozen seats at least.' Pausing, he seemed more amused than angry, a circumstance which caused Keri some astonishment. 'On one seat, right at the front of a long patio, was rather beautifully carved the name of Rochdale Football Club.'

141

'Oh, dear. . . .' She looked ahead, distresed and more ashamed than ever. 'I don't know what to say,' she added apologetically, and Paul surprised her even more by actually bursting out laughing. 'You surely don't consider it funny,' she said in a faintly censorious tone.

'Not in the least; nevertheless, it's not much use my bemoaning the fact, is it?'

'That's one way of looking at it,' she was forced to agree, subconsciously comparing this man with the stern austere partner she had encountered when she had attempted to assert her authority. Perhaps, she decided, she should have adopted a different approach altogether, a more careful and accommodating approach, having in mind her prior knowledge that Paul von Hasler, even at the age of twenty, was the severe, inflexible type of man.

He was speaking again, chatting about the customs and the various celebrations which occurred in Switzerland.

'August the first is our national day and you'll see bonfires up on the hills, and flags flying everywhere.'

'I'm looking forward to that. The people wear their national costume and you have bands playing and dancing. Doug has told me all about it.'

'Doug?' Paul's tone appeared to harden slightly. 'You're very friendly with him, you told me?'

'We have become friendly, yes.' Keri hesitated a moment and then, 'Do you know him, Paul?'

'Naturally I know him——'

'I meant, do you know him well?'

'Not particularly well,' he frowned. 'Why do you ask?'

'It wasn't for any particular reason,' Keri hastily assured him, 'but he seems to know most of our employees fairly well.'

'He's been around for so long, that's why. I expect he knows employees from other hotels too—especially those in Interlaken.'

'Do you like him?'

'Good lord, why on earth should I?' Arrogance now, and yet it was no more than a return of Paul's customary manner.

'I merely wondered,' she returned rather lamely.

'Are you trying to ask me if I trust him?' Paul queried after he had spent a few seconds in concentration as he negotiated a dangerous bend. 'You're not thinking of becoming seriously attached, are you, Keri?'

'No—of course not!'

He smiled then and his manner underwent another change as the more approachable side of his nature came to the surface.

'That was vehement enough to convince anyone,' he told her with a laugh. A long silence followed before he asked, 'Are you intent on remaining single, and developing into a super-efficient hotel boss?'

'What makes you ask that?' She was thinking of her discovery and wondering what Paul would do if he were to learn that she cared for him.

'I suppose I was thinking about your parents,' he replied gently. 'Sometimes, when one is disillusioned in the way you must have been, one is put off the idea of marriage.'

'Nothing like that would put me off.' Keri spoke softly, and there was a sad yet musical note in her tone which brought her companion's head round swiftly. She saw the odd expression enter his eyes before he returned his attention to the road. 'I have sufficient confidence in myself to know that, given the opportunity, I could make a success of marriage.'

Paul became thoughtful, considering this.

'You have the right ideas, Keri, and I admire you for your determined spirit.'

'Even when it clashes with yours?' she could not help saying, and another laugh escaped him.

'We haven't had any real quarrel, have we, Keri?'

'You're evading the question.' But she too was laughing. She was happy, carefree; the sun was shining and she was not only where she wanted to be—with Paul—but she was seeing her partner in a most attractive light. The efficient man of business was gone and in his place was a most attractive holiday companion. For she regarded this trip as a holiday even though its function was to enable her to see her other properties.

'I admit it,' he replied, much to her surprise. 'You see, my dear, I don't want us to have any arguments on this trip.'

'So you, too, are regarding it as a break from work?'

'A holiday? Yes, I am, rather.'

'I suppose your main holiday is taken in the winter?'

'I usually go away in October, when things quieten down at the Schloss Raimegen. We are open for Christmas, as you know, so I like to be around at that time.'

'Where do you go for your holiday?'

'I have been to America on a couple of occasions, and to England, of course. But I prefer to go to some sunny, exotic place like the islands of the Caribbean.'

Keri's eyes shone. In those not-so-far-back days when she had been living from hand to mouth she had dreamed of a holiday in Barbados or St Kitts or one of the other islands that occupy that beautiful sea. Now, such a holiday was possible and without thinking she

144

said, turning eagerly to him,

'I'd love to come with you if you decide to go this year——' She stopped, flushing painfully. 'I'm sorry, Paul—take no notice of that! I spoke impulsively b-because I'd just realized th-that I can have a holiday of that kind.' She looked down at her hands and hoped he would not turn his head and see her heightened colour. But he did turn, and he even slowed down so that he could give a little more attention to her.

'Keri, I would like very much to have you with me. We shall discuss it and then I can see the travel agent about a booking.'

'You don't mind having me with you—oh, but no! You're just being polite and accommodating!'

'Dear Keri,' he laughed, 'have you ever known me to be accommodating in circumstances that are not wholly pleasing to me?'

This was spoken in tones of amusement, but the question itself was sufficient to assure her that Paul really did favour the idea of their taking a holiday together.

'No, I haven't, Paul,' she answered softly, and received the immediate response,

'Well then, why do you assume that I'm being accommodating now?' and without giving her the time to answer, 'As I've just said, I shall very much like having you with me.' Something in the timbre of his voice sent her pulses racing, and she sat back in her seat, hoping that this would help to restore her calm. And in the silence that followed she had time to reflect on Paul's attitude, on the dramatic change in his treatment of her, on the ready smiles and more especially in the tone of voice he had just used. Was he coming to like her—to regard her in any other light than that

145

of his partner? 'You're very quiet,' she heard him say at length. 'Are you sleepy or merely enjoying the drive?' They were just leaving Brienz, having driven along the northern shore of the lake where, from the impressive watershed, numerous streams danced their way over rocky beds to join the smooth blue waters of the ribbon lake.

'I'm enjoying the drive—very much indeed.' Her voice was light and her smile spontaneous. Paul, twisting his head, seemed in this one brief glance to be taking in the fact that she was happy, and his eyes flickered with an odd expression which she was able to note before he turned swiftly away again. What was he thinking? Why was he repeatedly turning to glance at her?

'I'm glad, Keri. And I hope that, when we are back home again, you'll be able to say that you've enjoyed the whole trip.'

She said nothing and for a long while there was silence in the car. But at last they were nearing the town and Paul began telling her about it, explaining that it was the capital of the Canton of that name.

'The monks built a village close to where the River Reuss emerges from the lake,' he said, 'and later this village developed into a market town. Today, Lucerne is one of the most popular holiday resorts of the Continent.' They were driving along the lakeside and Keri looked out on a scene of blue water and yachts with shining white sails. Many colourful rowing boats were sailing on the lake and several steamers were moored by the piers.

'It's no wonder it's popular,' remarked Keri appreciatively. 'It's beautiful!'

'We're almost there,' Paul told her, having merely smiled in response to her enthusiastic statement. 'Just in time for coffee.'

She was a trifle apprehensive now, wondering how the manager of the hotel would receive Paul's new partner. She mentioned this to him and he did no more than shrug his shoulders and say casually,

'Emil will have no alternative than accept you. He knew, on the death of your father, that you might be coming over to take your place in the business.' He was slowing down, and soon he turned into the long avenue which led to the front of the hotel. Trees and flowers in profusion lent colour and character to the grounds which swept away towards the woodlands beyond.

'It's modern, but very beautiful,' was Keri's comment as, having come from the car, she glanced around while she waited for Paul to collect a briefcase and other items which he had put on the back seat.

'You prefer something old, that's obvious.' Paul looked down at her as he reached her side. 'You've fallen in love with the Schloss Raimegen, that's for sure.'

Keri nodded her head, looking up into his face, producing a fluttering smile and hoping her eyes did not reveal one small degree of what was in her heart.

'Yes, I have fallen in love with the castle. I think it all began many years ago, when Father brought me over for a visit.'

'In those days when you were a little hooligan— yes, I remember.'

She coloured hotly.

'I didn't expect you to remind me of that,' she admonished him, and turned sharply away for her colour was rising all the time.

'Just how long did you remain such a little horror?'

147

he wanted to know as together they walked from the car to the hotel entrance. 'It's amazed me that your father had not crushed your spirit even before you were old enough to show any.'

'He was strict,' she agreed, 'but somehow I managed to have a will of my own.'

'Which you meant to assert when you came out to claim your inheritance,' he laughed. 'Well, I suppose I couldn't blame you, Keri, and as I mentioned the other day, I should have been far more understanding than I was.'

Surprising words for a man like Paul, she thought, but had no time to dwell on them at present, for the manager of the hotel was in the foyer, waiting for them, and he extended a hand immediately upon Paul's making the introduction.

'Miss Hartnell, I'm very happy to meet you!'

'How do you do,' she murmured, putting her hand into his. She had not expected to find so young a man as Emil Lauener who, she estimated, was still well under thirty.

'Coffee, Emil, would be most welcome,' said Paul, putting down the briefcase and other items on a small table on which there was a lamp and an ashtray. 'And then we shall get down to the business of showing Miss Hartnell around.'

'Very good, Herr von Hasler. Coffee first and work later!'

'We'll go into the lounge.' Paul took Keri's arm and steered her gently towards the open door leading from the foyer into a high-ceilinged, beautifully-decorated room where thick-pile carpet, wall-paintings, expensive furniture and an abundance of flowers all combined to produce a picture of luxury and good taste.

'Your father never liked this particular hotel,' he told her, pulling out a chair for her to sit down. 'He vowed at first that he would not put any money into it.'

'What a lot of trouble you must have had with him,' returned Keri with a grimace. 'How did you bring him round, then?' Her lovely eyes were enquiring as they watched his expression become a trifle grim. He sat down opposite to her and tapped a finger reflectively on the table.

'I remember we had a very heated argument about it. You see, I'd had an option on the place, but there was another prospective purchaser. Your father maintained the expenditure was not merited, but I, seeing the possibilities, was determined to have it. I won in the end—I rather think I threatened to bring the partnership to an end or some such thing.'

'You thought of bringing it to an end?' she asked him swiftly, and he smiled with a sort of grim humour.

'Dozens of times,' was his brief reply, and Keri could not help but remember that she herself had brought him to the point where he wanted to terminate the partnership. He had advised her to see her solicitor but later for some reason had become less interested in buying her out. And now he appeared to be totally resigned to having her as his partner. Fleetingly she allowed her thoughts to wander to what Doug was doing, but as this interlude was far too precious for her to let anything mar it she straightway dismissed all troublesome reminders of the mystery, and of such objectionable people as Gena and Ernst.

CHAPTER NINE

By half-past seven that evening Paul was driving into Basle, having introduced Keri to five managers already, and now she was to meet the sixth, Curdius Roth, manager of the Hotel Grand Stella, who had been expecting them to arrive about five in the afternoon. But the business had been time-consuming in that Keri, keenly interested to know all there was to know, had asked more questions than even she herself had expected. The result was that each interview had taken longer than Paul had originally estimated it would and therefore they were arriving in Basle more than two hours later than would otherwise have been the case.

'It's all my fault, isn't it?' Keri said apologetically when on arrival at the hotel in Basle Paul suggested they leave all business talks until the following morning. 'I shouldn't have been so curious about everything.'

'Interested,' he corrected mildly. 'Of course you did right in asking questions; it was expected of you.'

She had to laugh at this.

'I'm sure it wasn't, Paul. Why, you looked so surprised at some of the things I wanted to know.'

'Pleasantly surprised, my dear.' He was parking the car and when it actually came to a standstill he turned to her and added, 'You mustn't blame yourself for our being late on arrival here. We have plenty of time, Keri, and if it takes an extra day then why worry?'

'You don't mind? I thought you wanted to get back to the castle as soon as possible?'

'There's no desperate hurry,' he returned casually.

'The place can be run without my help.' He opened his door and slid from the seat. Within seconds he was opening Keri's door for her and she got out.

'Thank you,' she said with a sudden incomprehensible return of her shyness. 'This looks very imposing.'

'All our hotels are imposing, in their different ways.' He spoke quietly, but with an edge of amusement to his voice as he added, 'I'm glad you approve of our property.'

She looked swiftly at him, wondering if she would see a hint of mockery on his face, but he was smiling and her heart caught. He was far too attractive; it was no wonder she had fallen in love with him.

'I think that your father must have been a very clever man to have bought all these lovely hotels. His choice was excellent.'

'Your father was his partner, Keri. They were both clever men.'

'I wish I had known him better,' she said with a hint of regret. 'You were of the opinion that he was a lonely man, weren't you?'

'I'm sure he was lonely.'

Keri sighed and, hearing her, Paul became a trifle stern, stating firmly that she must never blame herself in any way as it was her father's own fault that he was lonely.

'Come,' he added briskly, 'let us forget such things and enjoy our dinner. We have an excellent chef here.'

An hour later, having been introduced to Herr Roth, Keri was sitting opposite Paul in the hotel restaurant, her face aglow with happiness, a circumstance that could not possibly escape her companion and he asked the reason for it.

'I'm just—er—excited, that's all,' she parried,

hoping that this would satisfy him and that he would not pursue the matter. But she was wrong.

'Excited about what?' he asked, watching her with an unreadable expression in his eyes.

Keri spread her hands, hoping the gesture would appear casual.

'The meeting of all those managers, and seeing the hotels. . . .' She tailed off a little lamely and Paul finished for her,

'And realizing that you owned half of everything that you saw?'

She coloured enchantingly and his eyes flickered with undisguised interest. She fluttered her lashes, feeling embarrassed by his stare and hoping to conceal her expression. Her lashes were long and dark and they cast shadows on to her cheeks.

'I don't think I was very concerned about that side of it,' she answered with perfect truth.

'You blush delightfully,' was his astounding comment, and she knew that he hadn't been listening to what she had said. Aware of his continued regard, she had to glance up at last . . . and what she saw in his eyes sent her pulses wildly racing, as they had raced once before today. She swallowed hard, unable to find anything to say, and, taking pity on her, Paul eased the tension by laughingly apologizing for the personal remark he had made. 'It was enough to make you blush again,' he added softly, and almost tenderly. 'Come, dear, take a look at the menu.'

Dear. . . . Her mind thrilled to the word and her heart seemed to be banging against her ribs. It was exceedingly difficult to retain even a modicum of calm, but she did manage, by summoning all her forces of control, to appear cool and collected—or at least she hoped she did.

'I like the idea of smoked ham with fresh fruit.' Keri looked up from the menu to ask if Paul would recommend this.

'You'll enjoy it,' he assured her, his eyes running down his own menu which he held in his hand. 'The ham's cut wafer-thin and you'll be given paw-paw and figs with it.'

She decided on this for a starter, choosing wild duck with orange sauce to follow. Paul chose chicken and oyster salad, with steak Diane to follow.

'I think a bottle of Château Cos d'Estournel would be the wine to go with this,' Paul decided, lifting a finger to bring the wine waiter over to him. 'And for a dessert I recommend the honey almond fondue. Have you ever had it?'

'No, but it sounds wonderful!'

He merely smiled at this and gave his attention to the wine waiter. After this delicious dinner they went out on to the balcony for coffee and liqueurs, and after that they went into the ballroom, a high-ceilinged hall with a dais at one end where the musicians sat. Along the sides of the room were banks of flowers exquisitely arranged, and in front of these were small glass-topped tables each with a crystal candle holder in which burned a coloured candle.

Paul had suggested that they take a look at the ballroom before taking a stroll in the grounds, but, once there, Paul asked her to dance. Eagerly she slipped into his arms, her heart and mind thrilled to this new attitude he was adopting towards her. Surely he liked her —and in an affectionate kind of way. For he was not the sort of man who would in normal circumstances unbend the way he had done during the whole of the day. His voice was almost tender on occasions, his glances admiring, his touch gentle, as it was now, when he was holding her close to him because another couple had come rather too near.

'I think we can leave the business side of this until the morning,' Paul was saying after the third dance. 'It's late in any case.' He looked down into her eyes, noting their brightness and the fluttering of her lashes. Her lips were softly parted in a smile; her lovely hair fell on to her bare shoulders. Paul's eyes flickered, taking in every detail—the beauty, the movement, the all-revealing expression in her starry gaze. 'Do you want to dance again, or shall we go out on to the terrace for a while?'

'Whichever you want to do.' She spoke a little breathlessly, but she hoped he did not notice. 'I'm easy, Paul.'

He gave a soft laugh and, his arms around her shoulder, he guided her from the hall to the terrace outside.

'It's becoming rather overpowering in there. It's the busiest time of the year and every room is occupied.' He brought her a chair and they both sat down. 'You're not tired?' he asked as the thought occurred to him. 'Do say so if you are, Keri.'

She shook her head. Even if she were tired she would not have terminated this delightful interlude with Paul.

'No, I'm not a bit tired.' Her face was turned to him and she noted his keen interest—the intense scrutiny of those dark eyes, eyes which could be so cold and unfathomable but which now held a much softer light, matching the softer line of his mouth. Keri stirred restlessly, disturbed both by his stare and by the rapid beating of her own heart. Her throat seemed blocked inexplicably; she wanted him to speak—to end the silence—because she herself could not. The very air around them was tense; the idea of time and space was gone from her mind and she felt as if she were suspended in some nebulous region between a dream and a reality.

Paul was speaking, his voice was soft as he talked about the rest of the trip, and what Keri had to see. She listened yet scarcely heard, for the word 'business' seemed grossly out of place on an evening like this when the moon was high and the river gleaming in its glow. Dignified old residences nestled along its banks, their lights twinkling like golden stars as they filtered through the heavy-foliaged branches of the chestnut trees which grew in such profusion.

It was almost midnight when, having said good night to the manager, Paul and Keri went up to their respective rooms. Outside Keri's door they stopped to bid one another good night, but before Keri could even guess what was going to happen she found herself in Paul's arms, and her face being gently tilted so that his lips could claim hers. The kiss was tender yet passionate, Paul's arms gentle yet possessive.

'Dear Keri,' he murmured, his lips close to her cheek. 'Sleep well, my dear.'

'Yes. . . .' She was all confusion and in a little nervous gesture she drew her fingers through her hair so that it was scraped back against her head.

'Leave it,' he said, taking hold of her hand and clasping it in his. 'You have the most beautiful hair I have ever seen,' and taking it in his other hand he drew his own fingers through it, gently and caressingly. 'That's better; it's back in its proper place.' He was

155

smiling with some amusement at her confusion. 'I'm afraid I've disconcerted you,' he said, and Keri mentally put that down as the greatest understatement she had ever heard. 'But I would not have kissed you had I not been sure that no objection would be forthcoming —There, I've disconcerted you even more,' he laughed. 'Good night, my little Keri. You and I have something to discuss in the morning—and it has nothing to do with business.' And with that he was gone, leaving her with a heart as light as air and a firm conviction that she was destined for a sleepless night.

Paul bought the engagement ring in Geneva, after they had spent the night there, in the luxury hotel on a rise overlooking the lake where the River Rhône, reaching a width of over eight hundred feet, left the lake to meander away until it joined the Mediterranean Sea. The lovely height of Mont Salève rose above the town, majestically gleaming in the golden rays of sunlight streaming down from a cloudless blue sky. It was for Keri the most perfect day she had ever known, and even when the ring was on her finger—a flawless fine-white diamond—she was scarcely able to believe it was all really happening—that Paul loved her and wanted her for his wife. She tried to discover how it had all come about, to pin-point the actual moment when Paul had realized that he cared, but it was not possible. But that it had happened suddenly he himself admitted, although he did tell her that he had, in one astounding moment, hated the idea of buying her out, and this meant, of course, that he was not so anxious for her to leave the castle as he had been previously. He had talked about the business with such confidence that practically all her fears were dissolved, and once again

Keri asserted confidently that Gena was all wrong; there was no valid reason for her assertion that she, Keri, had no right at the Schloss Raimegen; the girl was merely romancing, obsessed as she was with becoming the 'queen of the castle' as she so arrogantly liked to picture herself.

Keri could not help wondering what Paul would say were he to know of these stupid mind-wanderings of Gena's. Nor could she help wondering what Gena was going to say on learning of the engagement. That she would be furious and frustrated was certain and, surmised Keri, she would be sure to hand in her notice, in which case she would be gone within four or five weeks from now.

'Beloved,' whispered Paul as they were saying good night after having been out to dine at a restaurant on the lakeside, 'tell me you'll marry me soon—very soon.'

'Just when you say,' returned Keri obligingly. 'I have no ties in England—no relatives to bring out, as you know.' Inevitably her thought flew to her mother, whom she would not recognize were she to find herself face to face with her at this moment. 'No one of my own....' These five words were uttered in an almost inaudible voice, a husky voice and sad. Paul drew her close to his breast and she was comforted by his embrace and his tender smile, and his kiss.

'Soon you'll have a husband and, later, a family to call your own.' He held her from him, his eyes alight with love and tenderness, but it was amusement that edged his voice as he said, 'You're blushing, my love; how very shy you are!'

She laughed, a shaky laugh, and buried her face in his coat.

'You seem to like making me blush,' she complained,

157

but her voice was tender and low, and revealing all the love she felt for him.

'Do you blame me, when you do it so enchantingly?'

'I shall steel myself against your efforts!'

'I sincerely hope not, my love, since that shy, sweet colour delights my eye.'

She laughed again, this time with him. And then they were close and he was kissing her good night.

'Tomorrow we have two calls to make and then—home!'

'Back to our castle on the hill!'

'You can begin making arrangements for your dress to be made. Luise will tell you of a dressmaker.'

'In Wilderswil?'

'No, in Bern.' Paul bent his head to touch her lips with his. 'Keri, sweetheart, I must let you go.'

'Yes. Good night, dearest Paul. I love you.'

His eyes became tender as he heard these words.

'I'm rather glad about that,' he returned before, with a little sigh of regret, he released her and, opening her bedroom door, allowed her to pass inside. The door closed softly and he was gone.

'I must be the happiest girl in Switzerland!' With a lift of her long full skirt she swirled round and round on the bedroom floor. 'Wait until I tell Doug! Won't he be surprised?—won't everyone be surprised?'

Afterwards, whenever that night came back to her Keri could not understand how she could have been so completely intoxicated by happiness that she could lightly put aside the mystery which a few days previously had loomed so large and fearsome. It was as if she had entered a realm of safety simply because she was engaged to Paul, a realm where nothing could touch either of them, where a girl called Gena—if she did exist at all—was nothing more troublesome than a shadow, and a temporary one at that. For the shadow would be removed without very much effort or delay.

So much for her wishful thinking! It was Gena's voice which brought Keri right back to earth, and to reality, where danger spread its black wings between her and the cloudless dream-world in which she had been living.

'So you and Paul are engaged to be married?' The grating voice came to Keri when she was in the castle garden, only a couple of hours after she and Paul had arrived back from their trip. She had gone up to her room, leaving Paul to spread the news, and although she had known that Gena would receive that news with a gnashing of teeth, as it were, she was not prepared for what the girl would say to her immediately an opportunity presented itself.

Keri had come down later in the afternoon and had decided to occupy herself with putting fresh flowers on to the tables in the dining-room. The vases were small and dainty and the task of cutting small flowers was a most pleasant one which Keri was thoroughly enjoying, when the voice of Gena broke into this tender task and Keri straightened up, a bunch of pansies in her hand.

'What a fool you are! You shall never marry him— never! Do you understand?' The beautiful face was twisted out of all recognition, the dark eyes smouldering like embers about to break into flame. Her hands were clenched at her sides, and her chest was heaving as if she were out of breath. 'I told Ernst that I ought to have enlightened you! That was when I saw you going off with Paul! Yes, I should have let you know everything long before now....' The girl came close and her face, still twisted into lines of black hatred, almost touched Keri's for one fleeting moment before, disgusted and yet trembling with fear, she stepped hastily backwards, out of Gena's way. 'You, my girl, have no right in this castle! You don't own any part of it, or of the business as a whole——'

'Gena!' It was Ernst and his voice was cracked and hoarse. 'You fool, Gena! You have no sense at all——'

'Mind your own business! She's got to know—and now!'

'No!' Ernst gripped her arm, but she twisted away, her eyes bulging like those of a woman demented. 'Gena....' Ernst stopped for a second and then spoke in German. And what he said obviously went right home, for Gena seemed to make a tremendous effort to collect herself and, without even a backward glance at Keri, she allowed herself to be led away towards a quiet seat under a tree at the far end of the grounds. White to the lips, and trembling all over, Keri watched the couple until, reaching the seat, they sat down. They were a good distance away, but she could still feel the evil presence of the girl, and of her dark eyes boring into her. Picking up the one or two flowers that had fluttered down from her trembling fingers, Keri walked unsteadily to the side entrance of the castle, as it was nearer than the front door. She had to pass the porters' room and just as she came abreast of the door it opened and Bill stood there.

'I was just coming to look for yer, Miss Hartnell,' he said in a low and guarded tone, while his eyes looked around to see if anyone was about. 'A friend of yours— Mr Doug—were speaking ter me—asking questions, like. And then 'e said as I was ter give you a message.'

'Yes,' she prompted breathlessly, 'what is the message, Bill?'

'Youse ter meet 'im in restaurant 'ere in Wilderswil —on corner of crossroads. Yer knows it?'

'Yes—yes, I do. When have I to meet him?' She was very white and quite unconsciously she swayed towards him. His hand came out instantly, and supported her. She allowed it to remain under her arm, was in fact grateful for it.

'Are yer all right?' he asked in some concern, his eyes searching her face.

'Yes, of course——'

'I don't think you are! It's the excitement, I reckon. Eh, but I were pleased when the boss said yer were engaged. Lassie,' he said in a much louder voice, 'are yer going ter faint or summat?'

She shook her head impatiently, and asked again about the meeting with Doug. She was to be there at half-past nine that evening, Bill told her and then added,

'But if yer hadn't arrived back I was to phone 'im at half-past five today.'

'Thanks for the message, Bill.' Her relief was great, for she had not known where to turn, or to whom. She had known that there was to be a meeting between her and Doug, but as he was due to return to England in two days' time, she wondered how she could contact him before he departed, since it would be at least a week before he returned, bringing out another party who, this time, were to stay at an hotel in Wilderswil and not in Interlaken.

'That's all right.' Bill paused, undecided for a space, and then, 'Yer don't look at all well, lassie. Why not come in and sit yer down fer a bit? There's no one in just now as t'other porter's 'aving 'is day off.'

She still felt weak and drained and after the merest pause she said yes, she would go in and sit down. She wanted to know what Doug had been saying, for one thing, and for another she did not wish to bump into Paul while she was in this state of discomposure, for he would be bound to ask some awkward questions.

Kicking open the door with his foot, Bill shepherded her into the room and over to a chair.

'Sit yer down, lassie, while I get yer a glass of water —No, wait, I've summat a little stronger——'

'No, thank you all the same, Bill. Water will do very well. I've—er—a slight headache, that's all.'

'I dunno think so,' he argued bluntly. 'I knows that sorta look on your face. Youse in some sorta trouble, I reckon?'

She shook her head, but weakly. But had at one time been her only friend—when she and he had been victims of her father's meanness. Two persecuted people finding comfort in each other's company. Keri felt very close to him at this moment, regarding him almost in the light of a father, and the great difference in status meant nothing at all. But it never had, for Bill was no ordinary employee—even Paul owned to this. He was here for life and when the time came for him to retire he would still have a home, and a comfortable one at that.

'It's nothing you can help me with,' she told him gently at last, aware of his anxious expression as he gazed down at her from where he stood, close to her chair. 'I wish it was, Bill.' Her voice quivered, for she was terribly afraid—afraid for Paul and for herself; afraid for the future. For it did seem that Gena held in her possession some dangerous weapon which had the power to destroy.

'I ain't no fool, Miss 'Artnell, and I don't go about

with me eyes and ears shut. That was why I was able to tell Mr Doug what 'e wanted ter know.'

Her head came up swiftly. It would appear that she was going to receive the information she desired without having to ask too many questions.

'What did he want to know, Bill?'

'Drink yer water, lassie. I 'ates ter see youse looking so white, like.'

She took a drink from the glass he had given her, but her gaze was questioning and he began to talk. Doug had questioned him only after extracting a promise that none of this would be divulged to anyone at any time whatsoever.

'He didna mean you, though. Well now, Keri——' He stopped and apologized, searching her face to see whether or not she was annoyed at his use of her Christian name.

'You always used to call me Keri,' she smiled. 'There's no reason why you shouldn't do so now.'

'The boss wouldn't like it. 'Owever, if you're willing then why not? It's a deal easier for me, I can tell you.' He paused and she waited for him to continue. 'As I was saying, Mr Doug asked me questions, like fer instance what I knew about yer father and 'is character. Well, 'im being dead and gone—rest 'is soul—I wasna too keen on describing 'is character. But Mr Doug, he kept on and in the end I says what was in me mind. Then Mr Doug asks about Gena Curbishly and I then guesses that summat's afoot and that Mr Doug was working in yer interests. Yer see, I'd known all along that Miss Curbishly was mad at your coming here, and one day when I was in garden having decided to pull up a few weeds, I 'eard 'er and Ernst talking and she out and said as she was the rightful missus 'ere and she

163

wasna going ter 'ave another woman coming and taking over summat as wasna 'ers. Now, I ses ter meself, that one means Miss Keri, who definitely is rightful owner of 'alf the business, seeing as it were 'er father's afore 'er. So I listens a bit more and finds out that she knows a thing what'll get the boss into serious trouble. But I never did find out what it was, unfortunately. Mr Doug, though, he wags 'is 'ead all time I'm talking and I guess as 'e knows what it is.'

Keri, whiter than ever now, actually did feel faint, and she asked Bill for another glass of water. Anxiously he asked if he ought to bring Paul, but she shook her head vigorously.

'No, Bill, I don't want him to see me like this. Half past nine, you said, in the restaurant on the corner . . .?'

How was she to leave the hotel without Paul knowing? They were dining together, naturally, and it was to be expected that he would wish to spend the rest of the evening with her. But she must see Doug—it was imperative, and so, during dinner, she mentioned that she had a headache.

'Is it very bad?' Paul asked anxiously, his tender glance taking in her pallor. 'Shall I get you some tablets?'

'No, Paul. I think I'd better to go bed—when we've finished dinner, of course.' She could have cried at the disappointment on his face, but he very obligingly agreed that she would be better in bed.

'You're so pale, my love. What is it?'

She swallowed surreptitiously, lowering her lashes to hide her expression.

'I expect it's the excitement of the past few days.' And she actually managed to laugh self-deprecatingly.

'You must admit that there's an excuse for me to be a little tense and overwrought?'

'Of course, darling. How lacking I am in understanding. Shall I come up and sit with you?'

Swiftly she shook her head.

'I shall sleep, Paul. I'm so sorry. . . .'

'Don't apologize. I only hope you'll feel better in the morning.'

It had not been too difficult, she thought, when at a quarter past nine she was in her room, collecting a cardigan in case it was chilly when she was coming home. It was quite dark outside and she had no difficulty at all in leaving the castle grounds after she had managed to leave the castle itself by the side door. Doug was already at the restaurant, having obtained a table in a corner, behind a screen of bougainvillaeas growing in giant earthenware pots. She joined him— and saw at once that he had made some important discoveries. His face was grave—and apologetic. He was ill at ease and she knew instinctively that he was wishing he had not offered to investigate the mystery for her.

'Doug . . . what is it? What have you discovered?' she asked in beseeching tones. 'Tell me at once, because I'm sure something is drastically wrong.'

He ordered drinks and when they arrived he still had not said anything more important than to ask her how she had enjoyed her trip. She tried to tell him she was engaged to Paul, but the words stuck in her throat, because of Doug's own hesitant attitude, his air of guilt and regret. Twice she begged him to speak, but each time he brought the subject back to unimportant things. But at last he talked, and as he did Keri's eyes widened, and then became filled with fear.

'So Father left everything to Paul, and Paul destroyed the will.' She could scarcely speak for the fear that possessed her, fear for Paul, who had done this illegal action solely because he believed in fair play, believed that she should have inherited what was her father's share of the business. 'Gena actually saw him burn the will?'

'Steady on,' warned Doug. 'I've just told you of my *deductions*. They might be wrong——'

'They're not, Doug,' she interrupted in low and hopeless tones. 'It all fits so perfectly. Gena is intending to blackmail Paul into marrying her. . . .' Her voice trailed away as she put her left hand on the table. Doug stared, bereft of speech for one disbelieving moment before speaking the one word,

'Paul?'

'Yes,' she faltered, the tears rolling down her face. 'He asked me to marry him and he bought the ring in Geneva.'

'God—what an infernal mess!'

'I see now why you wanted to see the room—Paul's private sitting-room. You wanted to see if there was a fireplace in it.'

'Yes,' admitted Doug. 'From what I had already learned I felt sure that a will had been in existence but that Paul, with his clear-cut ideas about honour and fair play which you yourself described to me on my questioning you, had most likely destroyed the will. And as Gena had actually seen him do this it was almost certain that it had been burned. Any other form of destruction would be far too risky—tearing it up and throwing it into the dustbin, for example.'

'You've questioned Bill; he told me.'

'I wanted to know more about your father. When

Bill told me how he treated you after your mother went off I suspected that he would most certainly cut you out of his will. This he did, but it didn't go to charity, as you surmised it would. Had it been left to charity then Paul wouldn't have destroyed the will. No, it's my firm belief that Paul came into everything but that he wanted you to have your share—your share in money. So he offered to buy you out. In other words, Keri, he was making you a gift of what, by law, was his.'

Keri nodded, too full to speak as she thought of how she had treated Paul, demanding her rights ... when she had no rights. No wonder he was angry and impatient with her. Perhaps he had on occasions even begun to regret the gift he had made to her. 'You can see now why I said you might not be happy with the result of my investigations?' Doug spoke gently, compassionately, and he reached across the table and covered her hand with his. 'I'm so sorry, Keri, and believe me, I have no advice to offer now that you've become engaged to Paul. Had your own attitude continued to be one of indignation at the way he was treating you I could have suggested you sell out to him——'

'Sell out? It isn't mine to sell.'

'Paul considers it's yours, my dear.' Keri said nothing, but just stared dumbly at him, her whole world having crashed, leaving her with far far less than she had before. At least her heart had been her own, whole and unscarred. 'If you remember, I hinted that there was another reason why Paul should have wanted to buy you out—this was after you had maintained that his reason was that he desired full control of the business. That second reason, Keri, was in my opinion, that having decided that it would be a gross injustice for you to lose everything he did, in his own way, en-

167

deavour to put things right by handing over to you a sum of money equal to a half share in the business.'

'Yes, I see it all now.' And so much more, she reflected as numerous incidents stood out before her, incidents which at the time of their occurrence were so frustratingly unfathomable. 'Paul would even risk imprisonment in order that I should have a fair deal.' She looked at Doug, misty-eyed and drawn. 'It just proves how wonderful he is. I was right when I told you he was an honourable man.'

Doug nodded his head.

'Undoubtedly he is an honourable man.'

'It wasn't as if he knew me properly. . . .' Her memory brought back to that first day, when she had gained the impression that Paul was making an assessment of her character, trying to decide whether or not he had made a correct decision. She had thought it so strange at the time, but now—how well it all fitted in! For she could see that this was exactly what he had been doing—asking himself if he had done the right thing in destroying the will that left everything to him and nothing to her. It was feasible that he should be making an assessment, trying to satisfy himself that he had done what he had done for someone who deserved it. Guilt consumed her as she thought again of her own arrogance in the demands she had subsequently made. She looked at Doug and just had to say, 'If only I could put back the clock; I would never have been so haughty with him, reminding him all the time that as I was an equal partner then I would have a chalet, and help in running the business—oh, Doug, you have no idea what I was like with him! I'm sure that he often wished he had produced the will and claimed everything for himself.'

'I understand how you feel,' he returned sympathetically, but went on to add that no amount of self-recrimination would do any good now.

'No, I do realize that,' she quivered. Doug did not speak and her mind became reflective again. 'You know,' she murmured scarcely aware that she spoke aloud, 'I remember feeling a strange little tinge of agitation when on one occasion Paul and I were discussing this question of my being his equal partner. He mentioned that he had instructed his solicitor to explain everything to mine. It was so odd that anything *had* to be explained, and I remember feeling that all was not quite right—somehow.'

'I expect there have been more occasions than that when you have felt that all was not quite right?'

'Many occasions. And of course, there was Gena and her arrogant attitude towards me.'

'It's mainly because of Gena that I've told you all this, Keri,' he admitted. 'If it hadn't been for her and the harm she can do to Paul I would have kept my knowledge to myself——'

'Oh, no! I wouldn't have thanked you for that!'

'You would never have known, my dear. However, had it not been for Gena and her subtle implications there wouldn't have been any mystery, and had there not been any mystery I shouldn't have made the discoveries which I've made.'

'And as you say, I should never have known.'

'Where ignorance is bliss. . . .'

'Paul and I would have lived happily ever after . . . in our fairy-tale castle during the day and in his lovely chalet at night and at the week-ends.' Tears gathered in her eyes, but she drew out a handkerchief and wiped them away. And she managed to keep her voice steady and free from emotion as she told Doug about Gena's coming out to her in the garden that afternoon. 'It was after she had been informed about our engagement. She was like a mad creature, Doug,' she continued, and went on to explain all that had happened.

Doug was frowning when she had finished and he seemed puzzled in the extreme.

'It all fits except for one thing. Why was Ernst so determined to prevent Gena from divulging everything to you? There must have been a very good reason for that.'

'He must have considered that the time was not yet right.'

Doug shook his head, but almost immediately he was replacing this negative gesture by an affirmative one as he nodded thoughtfully.

'I believe that is the correct explanation. She'll speak to Paul first, so as to keep the secret in the family, as it were. She'll let him see that marriage to her is his only hope of escaping the law.'

'If I hadn't become engaged to Paul then she wouldn't have decided to bring things to a head just yet.'

'I believe she was ready to act, Keri. This mad obsession about reigning like a queen at the Schloss Raimegen was swiftly overrunning all else. She was becoming impatient, hence that other occasion when she had to be held back by Ernst.' Doug paused and then apologized again for his findings. 'But as I said, I just had to tell you, Keri.'

She looked at him, watching him take a long drink, saw the frown that creased his forehead and the expression of deep regret in his vivid blue eyes.

'Of course you did. You haven't a thing to blame yourself for. It would have come out very soon, as you

170

say.' She wondered if she was as white as she felt, wondered if her eyes reflected the great sadness that was in her heart. 'If you hadn't told me all then I would have been taken by surprise, and that would have been much, much worse than it is now.'

'I wonder if anything *could* be worse. If only you hadn't fallen in love with him—But what's the use of that kind of talk?' he said impatiently. 'What's done is done and nothing can alter it.' He took another drink and snapped his fingers for the waiter. He ordered a double whisky, and scowled when the waiter did not bring it right away. 'There's one thing which I don't seem to have put over to you,' he began when at last the glass was in his hand, 'and that is that all these findings are based on my own deductions, on the various scraps of information I've managed to extract from people working at the castle—Ernst was totally uncommunicative, by the way—and on what you yourself have told me. Gena could have been rambling——'

'You yourself said right at the beginning that she was quite all right in her head,' she interrupted to remind him, but to her surprise he shook his head and said that from things that had happened since he was now of the opinion that the girl's mind had been adversely affected by this overwhelming desire to become the exalted mistress of the Castle Raimegen.

He then went on,

'As I was saying, she could have been rambling when she said that she had a secret, a hold over Paul——'

'Doug,' interrupted Keri again, and now her voice was faintly accusing, and so was her gaze, 'you're not convincing me of anything. Your findings are correct. Paul found Father's will and he decided to burn it. Gena saw him, and then tried to get away before he could know this, but she got only as far as some point along the lobby. He came from the room, and he saw her there. Nothing would be said by him, naturally. And we know that nothing was said by her. But she knew that it was a will he had burned and I can only think that she was, at first, standing behind him when he put it into the fire——'

'One thing about all this that's puzzled me,' broke in Doug with a deepening of his frown, 'is how she knew about the will. It's not inconceivable, of course, Gena being what she is, that she could have entered Paul's private sanctum and blatantly read his private papers.'

'No, indeed! That's just what she would do. I would stake my life that she'd read that will. Why, everything points to the fact that she had read it.'

'I agree....' Doug took a drink, then flinched as if the liquid were burning his throat. 'Yet there are one or two loose ends.'

'Nothing of importance.' How calm she was! And cold—as if numbed by the catastrophe that had come to her, shattering all her lovely dreams and hopes and leaving her devoid of the power to think properly, or to feel. Yet she knew just what she must do—that was so clear that no doubts could ever overshadow it.

She told Doug that she must go away, back to England, and immediately.

'Leave Paul? No, Keri, you can't! He loves you and he'd be damnably hurt. You and he can get over this——'

'Better he be hurt than put in prison, disgraced for ever.' She was still cold and calm, but her beautiful eyes were filled with tears. 'Can you imagine Paul, so proud and so noble, standing in a court of law, being on trial for so serious a crime? Can you imagine him

172

being led off to prison——' She stopped and sought for a handkerchief. Doug handed her his. 'I wouldn't stay when, by my going, all that disgrace and discomfort can be avoided. Thank you, Doug, for all that you've done——'

'Keri, girl,' he broke in urgently and with a catch in his voice, 'don't act without thinking first. Talk to Paul; tell him everything—how you confided in me and how I investigated for you. Be totally open with him even though you might fear his anger when he knows what's been going on. He'll be warned then, and might be able to think of some way out of the situation. Tell him too, that he can trust me implicitly. I shall never breathe a word of all this to anyone. This I swear to you and am willing to swear it to him should he ask me to.'

'You're a very wonderful person, Doug,' she said. 'I believe you would indeed swear an oath for him, but it won't be necessary, because my mind is made up.' She looked at him through a mist of tears. 'This is goodbye, Doug; I shall leave the Schloss Raimegen first thing in the morning——'

'Leave the way clear for Gena?' he cut in, suddenly blazing with anger. 'Have you no fight in you at all?'

'I'm thinking of Paul,' was her quiet rejoinder. 'I love him dearly and it would not be an act of love if I stayed.'

Doug swallowed a lump in his throat. His anger had dissolved as quickly as it had appeared.

'Then there's nothing more I can say, Keri. Let me take you back, dear; it's getting late.'

CHAPTER TEN

DESPITE the fact that she had slept little Keri was up early and, taking out her suitcases, she began her packing. She wanted to slip away before breakfast, but when she gave this idea a little more thought she admitted that it was not possible, not without being seen, that was. There was Ernst on duty at the reception desk; there was Gena and Luise and Emma—all moving about, making preparations for the tours and other business of the day. Also, Keri wanted to say goodbye to Bill; he would not ask any questions, she knew, even though he would be extremely puzzled by her action in leaving the castle. And in addition to all this was the fact that Paul, having been anxious about her last evening, had said that he would have breakfast at the hotel the following morning, and he hoped to see her then. If she was not there he would send up to see if she was all right.

If it was only wedding nerves, he had said lovingly as he kissed her good night outside her bedroom door, then she would be all right again by the morning, but if she was not fully recovered then he would send for a doctor.

'Oh, no,' she had protested. 'I don't need a doctor, Paul!'

'If I decide you are not yourself then you shall have the doctor—No, my love, do not argue with me! The sooner you realize that arguments are futile, when I have made up my mind, then the happier you will be.'

He had held her close, kissing her tenderly before seeing her into her room. She must ring immediately if she wanted anything, he had told her. He himself was going to the chalet and so if she wished to telephone she could, he added. But, afraid that he himself might decide to phone, Keri stated firmly that she would be going to sleep.

But now she had the ordeal of taking breakfast with him and she did wonder how she could act normally when her heart was breaking. She was confused as to how she would get away and in the end decided to enlist the aid of Bill. He would know what to do; he would get a taxi and he would collect her luggage and bring it down to the hall. No one would question a porter taking suitcases to a taxi. Then she herself could just run out quickly and get in or, better still, she could meet the taxi at the end of the drive.

'Darling, are you feeling better?' This was Paul's greeting as he rose to his feet on her entering the dining-room. He was at a table just inside the door and Keri took the chair he had pulled out for her, managing a smile as she did so.

'I'm fine, Paul; thank you for asking.'

'That's very formal,' he teased, his eyes searching her face. 'Not shy again, I hope?'

She laughed, and thought herself rather clever for being able to do so.

'Not at all. But it's good manners to say thank you where a thank you is due.'

'I agree.' He was dressed in an open-necked shirt with a floral design; his hair was faintly awry and she concluded that there was a breeze blowing and that it had teased his hair as he came from the chalet to the hotel. He was so attractive that she felt an actual ache of love for him that dispelled for a time the terrible despair which had encompassed her since she had learned the truth and realized that her only course was to go away and allow Gena to become Paul's wife. But would he capitulate? Ernst had had his doubts. And yet, with the threat of exposure looming there above him, what could Paul do but succumb to Gena's demands? 'What are you having this morning?' Paul was asking as he took up the menu and passed it over to her. 'Eggs and bacon, or something lighter?'

'Just toast and coffee, Paul. Are you having something more substantial?'

He shook his head.

'I eat very little in the morning. I too shall have toast and coffee.'

Keri kept calm, much to her own surprise. She talked casually, smiling when a smile was called for, laughing when Paul laughed. Yet behind it all her heart was dying—slowly, painfully, for this was the last meal they would have together. And she was glad now that she had not been able to get away for here was a memory, precious and lovely; she would often in the long years ahead bring back her memories and this would be one of them. Memories.... How few there were, really, since she and Paul had only just come together—so suddenly, so unexpectedly, so naturally for all that.

Their breakfast was brought to them by a smiling Swiss waitress, a cousin of Luise who was a student on vacation, earning a little money which she intended to spend later on a holiday in France.

'What are you going to do now?' Paul wanted to know when, their meal over, they were preparing to leave the dining-room. 'I shall be free after lunch, so if you would like to go off on a shopping spree I shall be delighted to be your chauffeur!'

'That will be lovely! Yes, dear Paul, I would love to

go shopping.'

'Bern or Zürich?'

'I think Zürich, because I haven't shopped there yet.'

'Zürich it shall be. Your wishes shall be put before all else.' He laughed with her, noting the sparkle in her eyes and the flush which so enhanced the clear peaches and cream skin. 'My dearest Keri,' he murmured close to her ear as they sauntered along the passageway leading from the dining-room, 'I adore you!'

She laughed, when the tears were so very close, a tinkling laugh that sounded faintly shy, yet happy.

'And I love you, Paul. Remember that—always—always!'

He frowned then, and stopped to stare searchingly into her eyes.

'Darling . . . are those tears I see?'

'Of—of happiness, Paul. Surely you can see that!'

'Happiness . . .? Yes, of course I see.' But he was puzzled and in order that he should not ask her any more questions she made an excuse and, saying she would see him at lunch time, turned swiftly and ran from him, ran to the stairs. But at the bottom she turned; he had gone, along to the end of the corridor where his office was situated. Keri made for the other corridor, and for the porters' room. To her relief Bill was there. She told him what she wanted, her manner urgent, her voice slightly commanding.

'Hurry, Bill, I want to be away immediately!'

'Immediately, Keri? But why——?'

'Bill, I told myself you wouldn't ask me any questions; that's the reason I decided to enlist your help. Please do as I say—get a taxi and then take my suitcases from my room and put them in. If Miss Curbishly or Ernst—or anyone, in fact—should ask whose luggage you're putting in the taxi say you don't know the person's name, understand?'

'But——'

'She just asked you to fetch down her luggage! It isn't anything unusual, Bill. You scarcely ever do learn the names of the guests here.'

'No, that's right. But—lassie, what are yer a-doin' —running off like this when youse just gotten yourself engaged to the boss? I can't see as you've 'ad a quarrel already——'

'Bill, please do as I ask and don't waste any more time.'

'Well ... oh, all right, then. I suppose youse a-knowing what yer about. A taxi. I'll phone right away.'

'I shall be at the gate. Tell the driver to pick me up there.'

'Where would yer be going, Keri?'

'I can't tell you, Bill. I'm sorry.'

'I dunno like this business at all——' He scratched his head, looking exceedingly distressed. 'Mr Paul doesn't know about it and that's fer sure, and I canna say as I want to be around when he knows as youse done a bunk—left 'im flat—and fer no good reason as I can see.'

'Bill, it's for a very good reason. I can't stay. That's all I'm going to tell you. *I can't stay!*'

Muttering to himself, Bill went over to the telephone and as soon as she heard him speaking to the taxi company she whispered goodbye and, quietly opening the door, slipped out, hurried along the corridor and then, walking in a more leisurely manner, went up to her room to collect a camera and her handbag.

Gena was at the desk as she came down again. The girl glowered at her and yet there was also present in her eyes a distinct look of triumph.

'Going out to take pictures, Miss Hartnell?' she enquired insolently.

'Yes, I am.' She was glad the camera had misled the girl.

'I hope you get some good shots.'

'I hope so too.' Keri went out, into the sunshine—and she never glanced back as she walked, not too quickly, along the drive. Half way down she stepped to one side as the taxi came up; her heart seemed to be stilled, as if it rested after being held in the grip of pain. Footsteps behind her, hurried footsteps; it was Gena. She came alongside and spoke softly into Keri's ear.

'Bill has just brought some luggage down. I recognized it as yours——'

'You——!' Stopping dead in her tracks, Keri stared at her. 'How could you recognize it? You weren't about when I arrived.'

Gena's lip curled in a sneer and her dark eyes glinted with amusement.

'My girl, I make it my business to look around. Knowledge comes in useful sooner or later. I've been in your room several times, so I know those suitcases—brand new to come here, weren't they? And expensive; a pretty shade of blue with special locks. Tell me, why are you leaving in so dramatic a fashion? I'm intrigued——' She stopped on noting the look of contempt on Keri's face. 'I want to know! *I shall know*!' Eyes that glowed like fire and a mouth that moved spasmodically. Keri now had no doubts at all regarding Gena's mind not being all that was normal. 'Tell me why you're going! It's convenient to me, I admit, but how has it come about?'

179

'If it's convenient to you, then leave it at that. Paul will probably tell you, because I've left a short note——'

'Telling about me? Putting me in a bad light? Oh, but you shan't! I'll get the note—do you hear!'

'I have nothing to say to you, Miss Curbishly.' Keri, pale and trembling, turned again and slowly made her way to the end of the drive. Once there she glanced back. Gena had disappeared and Keri could imagine her going up to the room in which the note would be found.

The taxi arrived and Keri was about to get in when both she and the driver looked up on hearing a shout.

'Herr von Hasler,' murmured the man. 'I'll just wait to see what he wants——'

'No!' Urgently Keri stepped into the back seat and slammed the door. 'Move—please! I'm in a great hurry. I said move....' But it was too late. Paul was there, having run down the drive as fast as his long legs would carry him. After speaking to the driver in German he opened the door and, getting into the cab, sat down beside Keri.

'So you'd run from me without even an explanation?' No censure in his tone, as she was expecting, but to her amazement the tenderest inflection possible.

'Paul, I——' She broke off as the taxi began to move. It turned right round and within a few seconds it was pulling up at the front of the castle. 'I don't understand. Paul, I must leave you, I must, darling——'

'Out you get. Fritz, take out those suitcases and bring them in. Then find Bill and tell him to take them up to Miss Hartnell's room.' He turned to Keri. 'Come, my love, we'll go over to the chalet——'

'But, Paul, you don't understand. And how did you know I was leaving? I thought you were away from the hotel during the morning——'

'Darling, just do as I say. We'll talk in a few minutes.' He stopped because at that moment Gena appeared behind the reception desk, having come from the direction of the stairs.

'You!' She stared unbelievingly at Keri, then her eyes moved to Paul. 'What's going on? I thought she was leaving!'

'You hoped she was, Gena.' So soft the tone, but oh, how it terrified Keri. And his expression. He looked as if nothing less than murder was in his mind. Gena, eyes flashing triumphantly, snapped at him,

'Don't do anything to rub me up the wrong way, Paul. I can break you like that!' And in demonstration she picked up a pencil from the desk and broke it in two.

'Keri dear,' said Paul turning to her, 'you had nothing to fear. And, just to content you for the moment, I'll tell you that your friend Doug, feeling that you were acting foolishly, telephoned me about five minutes ago. I was over at the chalet and so you will realize that I've lost no time, And now, my love, we'll go over to our home and I can tell you the rest.'

'Wait!' Gena's imperious voice was raised, her face a deep purple colour. Several people who had just come in stopped to stare, curious as to what was happening. 'I have something to say to you, Paul! This castle is my heritage and I intend to rule here! You will be well advised to listen to what I have to say——'

'Ernst, if you value your job then take that woman away. I'll deal with her later. Ernst—*do you hear me*!'

'Yes—yes, Herr von Hasler, b—but I don't know if

she will come———'

Paul waited no longer but, taking Keri's arm, led her out into the garden and then across the lawn towards the secluded spot where his chalet was situated. Keri tried several times to speak, but she was too full and she abandoned the attempt. But once in the privacy of the lovely sitting-room of the chalet, sitting on the settee and with a drink in her hand, she felt much calmer . . . and totally confident that all was well.

'As I said, Doug telephoned, but it was not until you'd almost escaped me.' His voice was grim and so was his expression. 'It seems that he did not at first consider such a move, but eventually he did decide to warn me of the fact that you were leaving. Naturally I did spend a moment or two asking what it was all about and I was given a smattering of what had been going on.' He too had a glass in his hand but he made no attempt to drink from it. 'And now, my darling, you yourself can explain more fully.'

She looked at him, her mouth quivering. He smiled reassuringly and she began to speak. While she was doing so he frowned several times, and when she was explaining her own terror at the idea that he might be put in prison his anger was terrible to see and she felt sure that, had Gena been present, then he would have done her an injury.

'And so you see, Paul,' Keri ended, 'I had no alternative than to leave———'

'Doug told me he advised you to come and talk to me.'

Keri lowered her head.

'Yes, he did.'

'Had you done so, Keri, you would have been saved all this heartache, for I was never in danger of imprison-

182

ment, even though there did happen to be a will——'

'There was a will?' She looked bewilderedly at him. 'Then what happened to it?'

'It got burned——'

'You burned it—and Gena saw you?'

Paul frowned at this. He was standing by the settee looking down at her and shaking his head in a little gesture of impatience.

'Let me finish, dear,' he said, and then went on to say that, at the time of her father's death, a thorough search had been made both of his office and the private rooms he had occupied in the hotel. 'No will turned up and in consequence you inherited a half share in the business. However——' he paused a moment as if carefully choosing his words, 'your father did once intimate that he had made a will, leaving his share of the business to me.'

'He did?' Keri's eyes flickered with interest.

Paul nodded, and then,

'I explained this to my lawyer and insisted that he make it clear to your lawyer that I preferred to buy you out because, in this way, you'd have the cash, which was to my mind better than a half share in the business. I instructed my lawyer to emphasize this most strongly to yours.'

'Because you knew of the possible existence of a will, a will that disinherited me, and so you decided to give me the money right away. . . .' She looked at him with deep admiration, but he frowned at this expression and said,

'Look, Keri, don't get any ideas that I was acting from anything else but my own personal ideas of justice. In my opinion—and in anyone else's who believed in what was fair—the money was yours. It most

183

definitely was not mine even though, later, the will did turn up.'

'Disinheriting me. . . .'

Ignoring this, Paul said,

'One day, very soon after his death, I was working in my office and, opening a drawer which I used regularly, I found the will. I realized at once that someone had been tampering with my private papers——'

'Gena,' Keri could not help saying, and Paul nodded in agreement.

'We know that now, but at the time I had no idea who would do such a thing as to pry into my personal affairs. However, back to the will. Your father must have put it at the bottom of the drawer; this was done shortly before his death because otherwise I should have seen it sooner. Gena must have heard from Ernst that, in the absence of a will, my partner's daughter had inherited a half share in the business—and in this castle which, we also know now, was more important to her than anything else. And so she put the will immediately underneath an account book which I used every day, and which she knew I used every day because on one or two occasions she worked with me in my office, taking letters for me. She naturally believed that I'd be delighted to find the will which left everything to me, for it's obvious to us now that you were very much in her way.'

Keri merely nodded and Paul continued by saying that Gena had without a doubt read the letters which he, Paul, was receiving all the time from his lawyer regarding the offer he had made to buy Keri out, and it was reasonable to assume that Gena was anxious to terminate the negotiations which were being carried out beween the two lawyers. He then went on to talk about the will. 'It was typed out on a piece of bright green paper that had been torn off something—it looked like wrapping paper. It contained several typing errors, had no witnesses to the signature which itself was spidery and badly written that even I could not have sworn that it was his.'

Keri's eyes flickered questioningly.

'Do you believe it was his?'

'Yes, I do.' A long pause followed before Paul said, with quite obvious reluctance, 'Your father became a very heavy drinker, Keri.'

'He did?' She frowned, looking pained. 'You've never mentioned this to me before.'

'Nor would I have done so now had not all this wretched business come up.'

'So he signed the will when he was—drunk?'

'Most definitely; he also wrote it while under the influence of drink, for in ordinary circumstances his typing was perfect. He did all the letter-writing for the hotel.'

A deep silence followed, with both Keri and Paul sipping their drinks thoughtfully.

'The will,' she murmured at last, 'was it legal?'

'I was so sure that it was not legal that it amazes me that Gena should have considered it to be legal.' Paul went on to describe how it came to be burned. 'I had my lawyer coming the following day, so I took the will into my sitting-room and put it on the mantelpiece, having decided to show it to him first and then destroy it afterwards. However, later in the day I went into my room and, seeing it there, I took another look at it. This was when Gena saw me, apparently—and now I'm going on what both you and Doug have told me. I never saw her either in the room or in the open doorway. I was just putting the letter back on the mantel-piece when it caught the breeze from the open window and went into the hearth——'

'Only into the hearth?' she queried, her eyes flickering with interest.

Faintly he smiled, a measure of humour in his voice as he said,

'A piece of wood fell out as I bent to pick up the paper. I straightened up, suddenly deciding that I didn't wish to save it for my lawyer after all.'

'And so you let it burn?'

He nodded, still amused.

'I'm of the opinion that it was better that way, for lawyers can be so fussy at times. There might have been all sorts of complications and I considered I'd had enough from your father during his lifetime——'

'You made me a gift——'

'Not at all, Keri!' And now he was stern, masterful. 'The will was not legal——'

'But Father did intend you to have his share of the business,' she insisted. 'It's not a matter of legality, Paul, but the adherence to a person's wishes.'

'Your father did it to spite you, not to benefit me. We had never got on, remember.'

'No, but——'

'Darling,' he said rather impatiently, 'surely it's of no matter as things have turned out? As my wife you'd have had a half share anyway.' He sat down beside her and, taking her empty glass, put it beside his own on a small side-table. 'That eventuality escaped your father and for that we must be grateful, since had the idea of our marrying ever occurred to him then undoubtedly he would have left his share to a third person, with the most unpleasant consequences of our

186

having the new partner most likely coming here and making a nuisance of himself——'

'Just as I did,' she could not help saying guiltily. 'Paul, forgive me—I feel so dreadful when I look back on the attitude I took. It's a wonder you didn't lose your temper with me altogether.'

For a second he looked grim; then his expression changed to one of amusement.

'I did come very close to it,' he admitted. 'In fact, there were times when I could have resorted to the kind of treatment which had proved so effective several years before.'

She coloured vividly.

'That's not very gallant of you—to remind me of *that*!'

His grey eyes glimmered and his lips twitched.

'You did ask for it, my love, and if you ever ask for it again you'll——'

'Gena,' she broke in hastily, 'what will she do now?'

'Buy a ticket to England,' was the crisp rejoinder. 'Also, Ernst will be out of a job, now that I've heard all that you've told me about him.'

'He isn't as bad as Gena. I think we should give him a second chance.'

'He is going.' And this time Keri did not argue, for the expression on her fiancé's face warned her that it would be futile to do so.

'Isn't Doug a good detective?' Keri was saying a long while later as she stood, enfolded in her fiancé's arms. 'He learned from his cousin——'

'Good detective!' exclaimed Paul, holding her from him and staring into her glowing face. 'He got half of it wrong!'

'Not half,' she protested. 'It was just the part about

the will. He truly believed that it was a valid will that you'd destroyed.'

'Burned deliberately, you mean.'

She looked at him and said with a hint of mischief,

'Didn't you burn it deliberately?' and before he could reply, 'You've admitted it, so you really can't deny it, can you?'

Paul made no comment on this, but bent his head and she felt the tender warmth of his mouth on hers. And for the next few moments she gave herself up to the sweet joy of being in his arms, of feeling his strong lithe body pressed hard against hers and of his ardent voice telling her of his love.

March Paperbacks

AUTUMN TWILIGHT *by Anne Hampson*
Don Ramón told Lauren she should break her engagement and marry him instead. Should she take him seriously?

ISLE OF THE GOLDEN DRUM *by Rebecca Stratton*
It was bad enough being stranded on a Pacific island, thought Carys, without the added problem of the island's owner!

SATAN TOOK A BRIDE *by Violet Winspear*
How could quiet, convent-bred Toni marry a man like Luque de Mayo and expect the marriage to work?

A LESSON IN LOVING *by Margaret Way*
Rosslyn's small pupil was difficult—but so was the child's uncle!

LAND OF ENCHANTMENT *by Janet Dailey*
Diana was a model, Lije Masters a tough rancher—but they fell in love and married. Would Diana soon regret her action?

THE KILTED STRANGER *by Margaret Pargeter*
A surprise awaited Sue at the end of her journey to Scotland...

COME RUNNING *by Anne Mather*
Darrell had fallen in love with Matthew Lawford—who was married. How could she hope for happiness?

THE HOUSE OF KINGDOM *by Lucy Gillen*
Clay Kingdom ruled his business and his family with a rod of iron. Would young Sasha ever dare to defy him?

DEAR SIR *by Mary Burchell*
'Were you ever in Paris?' A lot depended on Alexa's answer!

SPREAD YOUR WINGS *by Sara Seale*
A winter in swinging London was a far cry from her country home—and would it make Gael any happier?

30p net each

Available March 1976

Also available this month, four titles in our Classic series

SWEET TO REMEMBER
by Anne Weale

When Clive Lister, rich and handsome, came into Deborah's life, John Harriby issued dire warnings about wolfishness. John was prejudiced, because he was in love with Deborah himself, but—could he be right all the same?

THE YOUNGEST BRIDESMAID
by Sara Seale

When Melissa walked out on him the day before their wedding Piers Merrick married her bridesmaid instead. Although it was a marriage of convenience, both Piers and Louise were prepared to try and make it succeed—but Melissa had other ideas.

MOON OVER AFRICA
by Pamela Kent

Elizabeth's journey to Cape Town included the very reverse of a shipboard romance, for a lively mutual dislike was established between her and a certain tall, dark passenger.

THE GARDEN OF PERSEPHONE
by Nan Asquith

When Stacey was widowed after a year of marriage, she felt that she could never love again. For her small son's sake, she went to visit her rich father-in-law on the Greek island of Melaenus and found herself offered, despite many complications there, the opportunity of another kind of happiness.

35p net each

Available February 1976

Your Mills & Boon selection!

Over the page we have listed a number of titles which we feel you may have missed or had difficulty in obtaining from your local bookshop over the past months. If you can see some titles you would like to add to your Mills & Boon collection, just tick your selection, fill in the coupon below and send the whole page to us with your remittance including postage and packing. We will despatch your order to you by return!

If you would like a complete list of all the Mills & Boon romances which are currently available either from your local bookshop or, if in difficulty, direct from Mills & Boon Reader Service, together with details of all the forthcoming publications and special offers, why not fill in the coupon below and you will receive, by return and post free, your own copy of the Mills & Boon catalogue—Happy Reading. Why not send for your copy today?

To: MILLS & BOON READER SERVICE, P.O. BOX 236, 14 Sanderstead Road, South Croydon, Surrey CR2 0YG, England

Please send me the titles ticked ☐

Please send me the free Mills & Boon Magazine ☐

I enclose £.............................(No C.O.D.) Please add 5p per book—standard charge of 25p per order when you order five or more paperbacks. (15p per paperback if you live outside the UK).

Name.. Miss/Mrs

Address ....

City/Town ....

County/Country........................Postal/Zip Code........................

Will South African and Rhodesian readers please write to: P.O. BOX 11190, JOHANNESBURG 2000, SOUTH AFRICA.
NEW TITLES ONLY available from this address.

MB 2/76

Your Mills & Boon Selection!

☐ 830
THE GIRL AT SALTBUSH FLAT
Dorothy Cork

☐ 835
FORBIDDEN RAPTURE
Violet Winspear

☐ 839
STARS THROUGH THE MIST
Betty Neels

☐ 843
CHATEAU IN PROVENCE
Rachel Lindsay

☐ 848
THE TOWER OF THE WINDS
Elizabeth Hunter

☐ 853
ENCHANTING SAMANTHA
Betty Neels

☐ 858
THE MASTER OF TAWHAI
Essie Summers

☐ 862
THE TREE OF IDLENESS
Elizabeth Hunter

☐ 867
FAIRWINDS
Rebecca Stratton

☐ 870
DARK ANGEL
Elizabeth Ashton

☐ 872
GALLANT'S FANCY
Flora Kidd

☐ 877
DANGEROUS WATERS
Rosalind Brett

☐ 880
RACHEL TREVELLYAN
Anne Mather

☐ 890
CONNELLY'S CASTLE
Gloria Bevan

☐ 893
THE FIRES OF TORRETTA
Iris Danbury

☐ 895
A PROMISE TO KEEP
Dorothy Cork

☐ 898
PEPPERTREE LANE
Linden Grierson

☐ 900
THE FEAST OF SARA
Anne Weale

☐ 906
STARS OVER SARAWAK
Anne Hampson

☐ 909
THE TARTAN TOUCH
Isobel Chace

☐ 911
ACROSS THE LAGOON
Roumelia Lane

☐ 915
NOT FAR FROM HEAVEN
Anne Hampson

☐ 917
CRUISE TO A WEDDING
Betty Neels

☐ 921
THE ROAD TO THE BORDER
Elizabeth Ashton

☐ 923
ISLAND OF DARKNESS
Rebecca Stratton

☐ 940
THE PAPER MARRIAGE
Flora Kidd

All priced at 20p. Please tick your requirements and use the
handy order form supplied overleaf.